Indomitable Spirit
by
Bernadette Marie

5 Prince Publishing
Denver, Colorado
www.5princebooks.com

This is a fictional work. The names, characters, incidents, places, and locations are solely the concepts and products of the author's imagination or are used to create a fictitious story and should not be construed as real.

5 PRINCE PUBLISHING AND BOOKS, LLC
PO Box 16507
Denver, CO 80216
www.5PrinceBooks.com

ISBN 13: 9781631120350 ISBN 10:1631120352
Indomitable Spirit
Bernadette Marie
Copyright Bernadette Marie 2014
Published by 5 Prince Publishing

Front Cover Photo by Antoinette Giambrocco
Cover design by Viola Estrella
Author Photo: Damon Kappel 2009

First Edition/First Printing April 2014 Printed U.S.A.

5 PRINCE PUBLISHING AND BOOKS, LLC.

For Stan,
My Indomitable Spirit is because of your belief in me.

To My 5 little Blackbelts: You inspired me long before you could kihap, kick, and take names. You inspire me every day. I love you all.

To my mom, dad, and sister: Every journey—businesses, books, or karate you were always there. I love you.

To Connie: Who thought we'd move from the parent chairs to the board room together. Thank you, for everything.

To Master Stephenie Becker: Thank you for sharing yourself with me. In your image I have created a strong, passionate woman who can hold her own...and love the man of her dreams.

To my karate family: Since the day my white belt was tied on me you were there for me. 8 years may have come and gone, but those bonds are still as tight as the knot on that belt. Tang Soo!

To Jester: Thank you for being my partner all those years and setting the bar so high. Also, thank you for giving me a handyman...one with a black eye and a sense of humor!

To Sara: Thank you for stepping in and helping me wrap this up! You too will continue to do great things with your indomitable spirit.

Dear Reader,

It is with great honor and passion that I bring to you this book. Many years of my life were spent training in the martial arts. Without that discipline and realized belief in myself so many of my dreams wouldn't have come true—including my writing career.

Indomitable Spirit is what Kym O'Bryne has. Left in the small town of Aspen Creek, she has been giving the unglamorous task of building the family's school. When she meets the less than cordial John Larson she assumes nothing good will ever happen when their paths cross.

As she gets to know John, and his four children, she realizes there is a lot to learn and a lot to give. And with an indomitable spirit anything is possible.

I hope you enjoy this Aspen Creek story. I look forward to bringing you many, many more.

Happy Reading,
Bernadette Marie

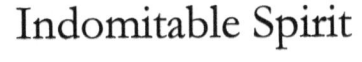

Indomitable Spirit

Chapter One

Crisp wind blew off the lake and down through the small mountain town. The streets were bare as the sun crested the mountaintop and sent the lake shimmering in gold and orange hues. Kym O'Bryne stood on her deck, wrapped in her heavy robe and fuzzy slippers, nursing a warm cup of coffee that steamed in the brisk November air.

She'd lived in many places. Korea, Ireland, California, and New York to name a few. Each place held its own mystique when fall began to give way to winter. But she'd never experienced anything like the change in the seasons in Colorado.

Already she'd been up for hours. She'd tended to her grandfather. In April he'd turned ninety, and though sharp as a tack, he was becoming frail. It had become her duty to take care of him and she did so with honor. She'd run three miles on her treadmill, within her warm house, and had trained in her dojang, which was downstairs from where she lived. She'd inherited the failing karate school for her thirtieth birthday.

Kym shook her head at the thought. She always assumed she'd run a school. What had made her father purchase the school and hand it over to her, she'd never know. It wasn't what she considered an ideal location. It was, however, her grandfather's dream to see his grandchildren carry on the family tradition. Though, when you saw the name O'Bryne on the door of a karate school, it didn't actually give the impression of traditional Korean training.

She shook off the cold and walked back into her home, slipped a piece of bread into the toaster, and finished her cup of coffee. Kym thought of her brothers and their minimal success with their schools. Both of her brothers, Ian and Liam, were Irish through and through. Ian with his blond hair and Liam with his red, both sported emerald green eyes like hers. They'd inherited them from their father, Todd O'Bryne of Dublin, Ireland.

She took her toast from the toaster when it popped and buttered it generously and then slathered strawberry jelly on top of it. It was her little bit of indulgence.

With her toast in hand she sat at the kitchen table, flipped open her laptop, and was pleased to find an email from her mother. She smiled.

Oh, it was a grand thought that Todd and Mi Sun O'Bryne had retired back to Dublin, where her father was born. Her mother sent a picture of them standing in front of a pub once owned by her father's family. They looked happy.

Her mother's name fit her so well. Mi Sun stood for beauty and goodness and that was what her mother always radiated.

Her parents' was a love story you'd have read in a book or seen in a movie. The tall, gangly Irishman who followed his wanderlust and landed in Korea, where he met the small, beautiful, and graceful daughter of a rice farmer. Both father and daughter dreamed of seeing the world. Todd and Mi Sun were married and lived in Korea for five years, where Ian was born. Then Todd took his family, father-in-law included, and moved to Ireland. That was where Kym was born.

Named after her mother's family Kym, Kym was born with the Korean features of her mother, except for the emerald green eyes she'd inherited from her father.

After five years it was off to America to live in Sacramento where little Irish Liam was born and the first school of the Kyms and O'Brynes was started.

It seems like a lifetime ago, Kym thought as she cleared her place at the table. She closed her laptop and moved to the cabinet to find the tea to make for her grandfather.

Now Ian, Liam, and she owned schools all over the country that taught Tang Soo Do to the masses, changing lives as they went along.

Kym, however, never thought her chance to change lives would be tucked in a small community in the Colorado mountains with less than three thousand people.

When she reached for the canister of tea, she found it was empty. That she should have known, it was on her list, but she'd forgotten to stop at the store. She wished she'd remembered, because the temperature had dropped at least thirty degrees from the day before and now she would have to bundle up, warm her car, and head out to find tea for her grandfather.

John Larson pushed through the front door of the Aspen Creek Market. How, he wondered, could kids eat through four boxes of cereal, two boxes of Pop-Tarts, and a box of frozen waffles in a week? They were going to break him.

He pulled out a cart, and with his head down, he started on his mission.

"Good morning, John. How are you this lovely morning?"

On a slight oath he turned to see Gloria, the cheerful clerk, standing at the register with her red apron barely encompassing her oversized chest and stomach.

"Mornin'." He pushed forward as quickly as he could. The last thing he needed on a Sunday morning was to be caught up in one of Gloria's hour-long renditions of what her grandbabies did this week that no other child has done before—like eat and poop. He just didn't need it.

He fretted over the cereals that his sons liked because there was a heroic character on them and then over to the ones with a princess, for his little Abby. But in the end he reached for the generic bag of cereal with the name that sounded name brand, but wasn't. He threw two different ones into his cart and with a grunt he took off to finish his shopping.

A woman's yelp made him shoot his head up when his cart collided with another. He found himself staring into the most mesmerizing green eyes he'd ever seen. How odd they seemed on the very petite Asian woman standing before him.

His tongue swelled in his mouth and he couldn't speak to apologize as she glared at him.

"Sir, don't you think an apology is in order?"

He stood there, staring at the long, dark hair that fell from beneath her sensible stocking cap, over her shoulders and down her back. It had been a very long time since a woman's beauty had rendered him unable to think or talk.

"Well, then I'll apologize for having my cart simply parked here in the way of your moving one." She huffed out, reached for a box of tea bags, and tossed it into her cart.

He simply watched as she backed up her cart and started around him. She stood erect, and, though she was probably only five feet tall, he thought she could easily walk among the city streets without anyone messing with the little ball of beauty and fire.

She stopped and shot him another look with those beautiful, cool eyes. "I haven't found too many people in this town who weren't treated to manners as a child, but I guess there is always a first." She went on her way, moving down the next aisle as John continued to get his breath back.

Once he shook off the utter irritation and delight of the little woman, John went back to filling his cart with things his children would, no doubt, devour before he got home from work the next day.

When he headed toward Gloria to check out, he noticed the dark-haired woman who had stunned his brain with just a few words walk out of the store.

He unloaded his items onto the conveyor as Gloria began to scan the boxes, bags, and cans.

"Where's your veggies?" she asked, analyzing his purchases.

"Pardon me?"

"Those kids need veggies."

"Yeah, I'll get some next time." That would shut her up for a moment, he hoped. Then he realized he needed information, and if anyone in town had it, it would be Gloria. "Hey, who was that woman that was just in here?"

"Oh, Kym?"

"Kym?"

"Just took over the karate school. Lives above it with her grandfather. Surprised you didn't know about it."

He shrugged. "Been busy, I guess."

"Heard. Fixing up Malory's bakery?"

"Yeah."

He wondered if he'd heard about her moving to town. Then again, people were always talking, and he was usually in his own world. There was too much on his plate to worry about town gossip. Until now.

He carried the bags to his truck and tossed them in the back. As he did he saw her, Kym, he reminded himself, dart out of Malory's bakery with a cup of coffee. No doubt it was one of those fancy blends that she'd brought in just for those who had to have it. He didn't see the point, but then again John didn't need anything that was fancy.

Kym hurried to her small Honda and drove away. John stood at the back of his truck and watched her disappear around the curve of the lake and behind the trees. It was a good thing she lived and worked at the same place, he figured. Sooner or later it was going to snow, and that little car wasn't going to go anywhere.

Wednesday mornings belonged to Kym. Her grandfather had made friends at the local seniors' center and on Wednesday there was always something for him to do there. That pleased them both. Taking care of him was an honor she did not take lightly. But still, to have the house to herself was priceless.

There were never any classes in her school until afternoon, and there were none on Wednesday. Sunday and Wednesday belonged to her; she saved her bookwork and her curriculum planning for business hours.

As she made breakfast she made a list of the things she wanted to do.

After her trip to the grocery store, she needed to drive into Grand Junction before the snow moved in and buy some loose tea. Her grandfather preferred it that way, though he'd never complain about a tea bag. Kym wanted to please him though and something as little as tea prepared the way he liked it brought her as much joy as it brought to him.

One day she wanted to go to Denver and do some shopping, and at some point, she'd like to make her way to Black Hawk and Central City and try her hand at the slot machines.

For today, she was going to venture around town and stick her head into the local shops. She'd been there a month and met only the parents of her students. More people knew her grandfather than knew her.

As she rose from the table, her cell phone rang and she was disappointed to find that the sign she'd ordered for the school was ready for installation. On a sigh, she realized she'd be giving up her Wednesday to work anyway.

The sign company had delivered her sign to Larson Hardware on Main Street. The owner, John Larson, had been contracted to hang it. However, she'd have to get in touch with him.

Well, she thought, there was no time like the present to stick her head in the door of a local business.

The hardware store was like many she'd been in over the years. Like a karate school, hardware stores had a look to them. Walls of hammers and screwdrivers met her, as well as the scents of paint and wood.

A woman behind the front counter was cutting a key for a man who stood tapping his fingers. He leaned over, rested on his elbows, and when he caught sight of her, he gave her a nod. "How's it going?"

"Oh, it's going well, thank you." She tried to plaster a pleasant smile on her dry lips that the bitter air was trying to ruin.

The woman turned off the noisy machine and slid the keys to the man. "Okay, Mac, all done." She turned her head toward Kym. "Oh, hi. Sorry, I'll be with you in just a moment."

Mac smiled. "Go ahead. I got time to wait."

"How can I help you?"

Kym stepped up to the counter. "I was told I could find a John Larson here."

"Sometimes you can." The woman leaned in near the man she'd called Mac and scanned her eyes over Kym. "He's on a job right now. Can I help you?"

"I'm Kym O'Bryne. My sign…"

"Oh." The woman stood up. "The karate gal."

Again, Kym forced a smile. "Yes, that's me."

The man turned full to her and gave her a long study. "O'Bryne? You don't look Irish."

"My father is Irish. My mother Korean. I take after her."

The woman walked around the counter and extended her hand. "I'm Kelley Larson, John's sister and co-owner of this establishment. This baboon is Mac Stern. Mac here coaches hockey over at the ice rink."

"It's nice to meet you both." She put pleasantness in her voice, as her mother always told her to do.

"John is working over at Malory's bakery today. I can have him give you a call."

"You know, I'll poke my head in there. I'm making my way around town today."

"I'm glad you stopped in." Kelley smiled widely. "You just let me know if you ever need anything. If I can't help you, John certainly can."

Kym thanked her and went about walking up the street toward the bakery. She looked forward to meeting a man of whom his sister spoke so highly. The wind was calm, but the air was still brisk. She pulled the scarf around her neck tighter and opened the door.

The smell of fresh baked bread and cookies washed over her as she shut the door behind her. The temperature inside was warm from the ovens and the obvious construction that was going on.

Malory's was one of the businesses Kym had visited every Sunday morning. The vanilla latte that she made was Kym's indulgence each week.

"Morning, Kym. What a treat to see you. It's not even Sunday." Malory Douglas waddled to the counter. Her extremely pregnant belly bulged beneath her apron.

The smile Kym gave Malory was not forced. She liked her and her bakery and was always happy to be there. "Actually I came on business. I'm looking for John Larson."

At that moment, a string of curses flew from the plastic tarp that was nailed into place and curtained the area between the working part of the bakery and the area Malory was having remodeled.

Kym's jaw dropped when she saw the man who walked out from the plastic wall. He shook his hand, which he'd obviously hit with a hammer.

"Wil, how about an ice pack?" He turned to Malory, but his eyes rested on Kym's. "Damn. Hi."

This time it was Kym that was stunned into silence. She'd spent her morning seeking out the very man she'd spent Sunday cursing for his rudeness. What had she done to deserve that?

"You two have met?" Malory asked.

"Not really. We bumped into each other Sunday morning," John answered.

"Bumped into each other? If I remember correctly, it was you who slammed into me."

"Now, I'm sorry about that."

"Really? I wouldn't know that. This is the first time I've heard you speak."

John shook his hand again and turned his stare to Malory. "Wil, the ice?"

"Be right back." Malory hurried off as quickly as her oversized body would let her.

"Do you always talk to women like that?" Kym fisted her hands on her hips.

He lifted a brow. "Like what?"

"Ordering them around and you don't even call her by her name."

At that he laughed. "Wil is her name. Her momma gave it to her before she died. Those of us who grew up with her only call her Wil."

Kym crossed her arms over her chest and shook her head in disgust.

Malory waddled back to them, a bag of ice in her hand. She laid it on his hand and he winced.

He slid a glance at Kym and then back at Malory. "Thank you, Malory."

"You're very welcome." She smiled at Kym and went back to her baking.

"See, was that so hard?" Kym tapped her booted foot.

"Why are you standing here giving me a hard time?" He shifted the bag from his hand and she could see where the bruise was already settling.

"Do you need a doctor?"

"For what? Because I hit my hand? Please. It's part of my life."

"That doesn't set well with me, knowing you're going to be on a ladder outside my school."

Kym watched his light blue eyes, hidden by the shadow of a ball cap with the name STANLEY written across the front of it, search for the connection. Then his head rose and his eyes widened. "You're the sign install?"

"Yes."

"Figures." He set the ice on the counter and worked his fingers open and closed.

"Listen, Mr. Larson, if you…"

"John."

Her arms were throbbing she'd been crossing them so tightly. She finally let them fall. "John, if you don't need the work, I can call someone else."

"I'll be there." He took off the aged hat and ran his hand over a mop of dark hair then as though expertly fitting it, he adjusted the hat until it sat perfectly back on his head again. "I'll come by around three. Once I get them settled, go by and get the sign, let's see—I'll need the bigger ladder, was it wired? No, no wire." He continued making his list aloud and Kym stood observing the many faces of John Larson.

The face itself wasn't unhandsome, though the day's worth of whiskers made him look tired and drawn. The flannel shirt he wore tucked into a pair of Wranglers and the belt buckle looked like maybe he'd won a rodeo once upon a time. If it weren't for the crease between his brows at all times, Kym would have thought he was a good-looking man. But his disposition left a haze over any handsome features.

John looked up as though he realized he was talking to himself. "I'll be there at three."

"Fine." Kym turned and left the bakery.

John set the bucket of tools in the back of his pickup. It was no wonder he'd smashed his hand, which still throbbed. His mind certainly hadn't been on his work for the past few days. It had been on Kym.

Why was it the woman could turn him inside out just by talking to him? Most people let him do what he did best, and that was build things. They didn't give him manners lessons about saying he was sorry, or how he spoke to people, or the names he called them. They most often left him the hell alone.

How come this Kym person was taking over his mind and time this week? He had better things to do than think about her and those beautiful eyes.

John shook away the thought.

Her eyes and that raven-black hair didn't mean squat. He had responsibilities and a job to do. Kids to feed. With a push, he closed the tailgate to his pickup, the sign securely placed in the bed, and headed toward the karate school.

When he parked, he could see her inside. There were no students. She was the only one on the blue-and-red rubber-matted floor. Even alone in the school, she wore a red uniform with a single, wide black stripe down each arm and leg. The belt tied around her waist was black with four gold bars embroidered on it. She watched herself in the mirrors that encompassed one wall.

Each series of moves started with her hands in fists before her and then, like a well-rehearsed dance, she'd move. Some moves were methodical and slow. Other moves were sharp and fast as though she were attacking. There were dozens of combinations she went through, and by the time John snapped back into reality he realized he'd watched her for over twenty minutes.

He walked back to his truck, yanked on his tool belt, and pulled the ladder from the metal racks that rose like a cage over the truck bed. He set it up in front of the door and went to work taking down the old sign.

He stopped when he heard the door to the school open below him. When he looked down there she was, barefoot and staring up at him.

Her hair was tied back and her eyes were more brilliant when not shadowed by that cascade of hair. John cleared his throat.

"Kinda cold to be without shoes, isn't it?"

"I consider it conditioning."

He nodded. He wasn't sure he'd met a woman quite as tough as she was, and that decision was made solely on the few times they'd spoken.

"I'll be up here a bit. You might want to watch for your students and have them go in the side door."

"I don't have any students today."

"Oh, well I saw you..." He stopped talking. The last thing she needed to know was that he was watching her. "I thought since you had on your uniform you were working."

"I don't usually work on Wednesdays. This one is an exception, thanks to the sign."

"The sign? Well I don't see you out here working on the sign. You could still take your day off."

Kym crossed her arms over her chest. "If you can't do the job, I can help you. However, I would think you are skilled in this area. And owning your own business, I would think you'd know you work whenever you please. So, today I chose to work on my curriculum and practice my forms for an extra hour."

"Extra hour? You've already done all of that once today?"

"Of course."

Her icy glare was telling him to stop talking, but it wasn't happening. "How often have you used that?" he asked as he twisted a socket wrench to loosen the bolt holding up one corner of the old sign. "I mean, really, do you get attacked a lot?" Just as he said it the wrench fell from his hand. By reflex, he slid down the ladder, even knowing he couldn't beat the tool to the ground. It was headed right for her head.

But as he landed, his calves and hands aching from the slide down the metal, he stood in astonishment. Kym held the wrench in one hand and had braced to support him should he tumble from the narrow sidewalk.

His heart pounded against his chest uncomfortably and it took him a moment to get his breath back.

"Did you get hurt? Did it hit you? God, I'm so sorry. I could have killed..."

Her gentle finger rose to his lips and pressed against them. "Being prepared does not always mean someone will attack you. You must always be prepared for the unexpected," she said in calm, even tone.

For the first time since he'd crashed into her at the store, he watched her smile. If he'd thought the eyes had already done him in, the smile sealed the deal.

Kym handed him back the wrench and before he could slide the tool into his belt, she pulled open his clenched fist.

"You hurt yourself when you slid down the ladder."

He looked down. Until that moment he hadn't realized how scraped up his hands were. Once he did, the ache and throbbing started.

He shrugged. "Not the first time. I'll survive."

"You'll come upstairs and I will fix your hand."

"I said I'm fine." He clenched the fist again and tried not to wince from the pain.

"You are one stubborn man, Mr. Larson."

He let out a grunt. "You're not the first to say so."

"If you won't let me help you, then you will suffer. Sometimes being strong isn't about suffering alone. Sometimes it takes a strong person to ask for help."

She turned and opened the door to the school.

"Hey," John called out after her. She turned back to him and he took a step in her direction. "I'm sorry I nearly killed you."

Kym only shook her head and went back inside.

John huffed out a breath, climbed back up the ladder, and cursed his aching hands.

"Finish the job, man. Then you can say goodbye to Miss Icy Stare Karate Teacher forever," he muttered to himself.

As he continued to work on the sign, he thought about her staring at him with those green eyes. When they were warm and friendly how would it feel when she looked at him? Damn, the last thing he needed in his life was a woman to make it more complicated than it already was.

Chapter Two

Kym could still hear John outside hanging the sign. With his hand injured the job was undoubtedly taking longer than he would have liked—or so she assumed by the language he was using.

Her grandfather had laughed as she had looked out the window for the tenth time in an hour.

"Go. Help."

"He doesn't deserve my help."

"All people deserve help," he said in his calm, knowing tone.

She'd never picked a fight with her grandfather, though she thought about it. There was no use. The old man would use that calm tone on her and it always went his way.

Kym took a breath to give her opinion again. Her grandfather closed his eyes and smiled. This was his way of shutting her out and making his words the last ones said.

She gritted her teeth and slowly let out a breath. The last thing she wanted to do was go outside and help the man who had been so obstinate—so rude.

As she looked at her grandfather again, his peaceful face had softened, but his eyes were still closed. Something was working in that head of his and she was going to learn some lesson from it—that much she knew.

Kym huffed to the front door and pulled her coat down off the hook. She'd changed her clothes. Perhaps it would put John Larson at ease. Maybe it was seeing a woman in uniform that had him acting so put off.

She slipped her arms though the sleeves of the coat and zipped it up. No, he'd been put off by her since he'd first seen her in the grocery store. There was a story behind the man's dark eyes and less than sunny disposition. Maybe he just needed a friend.

She opened the door and headed down the stairs to the school.

A friend—she thought about it again. He seemed to have those. The whole town knew him. Even Malory wasn't irritated by his snipping at her for help and that name he called her. Then again he'd said all her friends called her Wil.

Kym felt the familiar twist form in her stomach. She was the one who needed a friend. That's how it had always been. Her brothers made friends. They trained hard and played hard. She trained hard and then walked to a quiet corner and snuck away in a book. But friends weren't something she collected often.

As she reached the door she heard John let out one more curse.

"How's it going?" she asked trying to smile through her feelings of inadequacy.

"Am I making too much noise? Am I in the way?" he snapped as he cranked the wrench to tighten the bolt.

"No. I just thought I could give you a hand."

"Oh, since I hurt mine and can't seem to keep a wrench in my hand?"

"I didn't…" she blew out a breath. She needed to take a lesson from her grandfather right now. Calm your mind and your breath, she reminded herself. "No. I just wanted to offer some help."

"Sure now you do."

That snapped the calm. "I simply meant…"

John came down the ladder and looked up. "What do you think?"

It wasn't until that moment that she realized he had the sign hung and was done. No wonder he didn't take her offer of help seriously.

"It looks wonderful."

She'd never tired of seeing her family's name on signs. A lot of pride went into their schools. This one would be no different.

"Well, that's that." He turned and walked back to his truck where the old sign sat. "Do you want this one?"

She thought quickly. "No. Is there something you can do with it?"

It was just an old wooden sign which was so old all the paint and varnish had long worn off. "I'm sure I can chop it down. I can do something with it."

Kym nodded.

John began to load up his truck with the tools he'd taken out. Kym watched helplessly.

He moved back to gather his ladder and as he lowered it she watched him pull his hand back as if it hurt, but he didn't say anything.

John lifted the ladder onto the metal racks built up on the bed of the pickup truck.

"I guess that's all." He lifted the tailgate up.

"Thank you," Kym watched him clench his hand at his side.

"Doing my job."

On instinct she reached for his hand and held it up to examine it again. It looked horrible. The blood had dried, but it still needed to be bandaged.

"Please come in and let me fix this."

He took a breath to protest, but Kym did just as her grandfather would. She took a deep breath of her own and closed her eyes. When John didn't speak she turned, his wrist still in her hand, and walked into the school.

The moment she walked into the school she toed off her shoes. "You have to take off your boots."

"No."

She narrowed her eyes. How did her grandfather keep so calm?

"Mr. Larson, we do not wear shoes indoors. You leave the dirt of the world outside."

"Then I'll go back outside."

She clenched her jaw. "Please."

He rolled his eyes, shook his head, and then bent at the waist to untie the work boots kicking them off next to hers.

"Happy?"

She forced a smile. "Yes."

Kym walked to the matted floor, bowed, and started across.

"Do you expect me to bow?"

"I just expect you to let me look at that hand."

She was sure she heard him growl behind her, but she kept walking to the back of the school.

John had never felt so out of place in the town he'd grown up in. But following the little Korean spitfire he knew he was out of place.

At least she'd changed her clothes. The uniform she'd worn earlier had made him uncomfortable and weak. But in the pair of sweatpants with San Diego printed down the leg gave her a different look. A relaxed look. Her hair was piled high on her head in a messy bun and the T-shirt with the school's name on it hid under the large coat she wore.

If he hadn't been raised a gentleman, and if he didn't have four hungry kids at home waiting for him to make something horrible for dinner, he'd make a pass at her. But that wasn't John Larson.

No, John Larson was known for being an asshole. He wanted to laugh as the small woman pulled him through the back room of the school by the hand.

He growled more than he smiled. He snapped out answers more often than calmly explaining his situations. And he didn't laugh very often.

The more he thought about it he didn't like himself very much at all.

Hadn't his own sister told him that morning that he acted like a crabby eighty-year-old woman?

Okay, so this woman—nice-looking woman—wanted to take care of him. Was there anything wrong in that? After all he did hurt himself hanging *her* sign. And that was after *she* had him all riled up because he'd called Wil Wil. And what about that run in at the grocery store? That wasn't all his fault.

"Are you okay?" Kym asked.

"Fine."

"Then can you open your hand a little?"

He hadn't even realized that he'd tightened his hand so tight that the fist he made had his knuckles turning white and the cut on his hand bleeding again.

"Sorry."

Kym turned on the faucet at the sink, took a clean rag from a drawer, and wet it. She ringed it out, turned off the water, and turned back to him.

She took his hand, but this time when she grabbed his wrist he could have sworn she did something to him. His hand relaxed open and she pressed the rag to his raw skin. The first reaction was to jump, but he fought it. There was no way he'd show weakness to her.

"Don't take this off. I'm going to grab the first aid kit."

She walked to another cabinet and took down an enormous box.

"That's a first aid kit?"

She smiled and he'd never quite noticed that her cheeks rose high. Then again he realized she'd never smiled in his presence. Yep, he was an asshole.

Kym set the box down on the counter and began to look through it. "I'm prepared for everything. Sprained ankle, broken toe, sliver..."

"Sliver? You get slivers doing karate?"

There was a giggle. He'd made her giggle. "Sometimes you get slivers when you break boards."

Oh yeah. He was considering flirting with a woman who could break walls. That was a dumb idea.

Kym turned her hand over and showed him the scar on the side of her hand. "See that one? Now that was a sliver."

"You have a scar that big on your hand from breaking a board?"

"Six."

He forced down the lump in his throat. "Six boards?"

She laughed again as she took the cloth off his hand and set it on the counter. "To be honest I broke the boards first. I got the hunk of wood stuck in my hand when I was picking them back up."

His shoulders were tense as she took a gauze pad she'd covered in ointment and placed it on his hand. "You've been doing this a long time then?"

"Fixing hands?"

That made him relax. "Karate."

"I don't remember not doing it."

"O'Bryne? So your dad is Irish?"

"Yes. My parents have actually moved back to Dublin to retire. My mother is from Korea."

"That explains the dynamic eyes."

At that moment those very eyes shifted up to look at him through long dark lashes. "Dynamic eyes?"

Now he'd crossed the line. There was being nice and there was flirting. Then, his stomach growled and he no longer could think of the beautiful Korean and Irish woman before him. He needed to think about food and feeding others.

As soon as she finished wrapping his hand in gauze he pulled away from her.

"That looks good."

"Make sure it doesn't get infected."

"It won't." He was already tiptoeing over the red and blue mat as though it would turn into water or something. Once he made it to his boots he quickly slid his feet in. He'd never be able to tie them with his hand all bandaged up.

Quickly he opened the door and the cold smacked him. He'd grown too warm in the school with her touching him. Just as he stepped out onto the gravel he realized he was still an asshole—a big one running away.

It pained him, but he turned around and caught her eye from across the room. Those eyes were as magnificent from twenty feet as they were up close.

John swallowed hard. "Thank you," he said holding up the bandaged hand.

Kym didn't say a word she simply bowed her head gracefully.

He needed to get home. He needed the chaos of his family. He needed a beer. And when everyone was tucked in tight he needed a cold shower.

Chapter Three

Usually John would have stopped back by the store and made sure his sister had locked it up tight. But tonight he needed the chaos of his children to refocus his head.

His mother quickly shushed him as he opened the front door as she rocked with Cody in the rocking chair. He was nearly two, but he'd always be the baby.

"The middle two are playing in the bedroom, but it's gotten awfully quiet," she whispered.

John gave her a nod and headed down the hallway. It only took one whiff of the thick air to realize why they were so quiet. When he opened the door there was a four and six year old covered from head to toe in baby powder.

"What are you doing?" he asked too tired to yell or be really angry. He knew he had to pick his fights and he'd picked enough of them today with Kym O'Bryne. He shook his head. He'd come home so he could forget that. She wasn't supposed to be occupying his head any further.

"Look, Daddy. Mason is an old man," Abby said laughing.

John shook his head as he looked at his four year old son grinning up at him through white coated eyelashes.

"Mason, why did you let her do that?"

His son only giggled and that started Abby to giggle too.

"You two are trouble." He pinched the bridge of his nose with his bandaged hand.

"Dear, Lord, what happened to you?" His mother's voice came from behind him. "Oh, dear, what did you two do?"

"Mom, it just needs a vacuum. I can handle this."

She gave them a tsk tsk with her tongue and then reached for John's hand.

"And this?"

He pulled his hand back. "This is nothing. I hit my finger with the hammer when I was at Wil's and then I slid down the ladder when I dropped a wrench." *And it nearly landed on the most beautiful...* He bit down on the inside of his cheek to inflict just enough pain to occupy his mind.

"You're going to kill yourself."

"Not on purpose," he argued as he walked back down the hall toward the kitchen. "Where's Jacob?"

His mother only closed her eyes and he listened. He could hear the sound of the soccer ball against the wall in the basement.

"He's fuming?"

"He had a hard day at school again. He's just being constructive and using his anger to kick the ball around."

"How long before I have to fix that window again?"

She smiled. "If it helps, your father could come and put a board over it."

"I could do that too, Mom. Dad needs to keep relaxed."

He continued to the kitchen and she was right behind him. "You know he met a man at the rec center the other day. A Korean man."

That made John's spine straighten. "Really?"

"Yes. Something Kym..." she hummed as she tried to think of the name. "Anyway, his granddaughter owns the karate school. But he said he taught him some relaxation techniques and your father's been doing them. I think it's really helped his mood. You know he's been so cranky since his heart attack."

Yeah, he'd noticed.

John walked to the refrigerator and took out two frozen pizzas. His mother shook her head.

"Really? That's your dinner?"

"Mom, give it a rest." He tore open the packages. "Thanks for keeping an eye on the kids."

"It's what I can do to help."

"Well it means a lot." He pushed the buttons on the oven. "I didn't think it was going to keep being hard."

His mother rested her hand on his shoulder. "Until they are all raised it won't be easier honey. You have a lot to deal with."

"Great."

She sighed as she walked toward the back door and pulled her coat off the hook. "She wouldn't have left you on purpose."

John clenched his jaw.

"I'll be back in the morning." She kissed her fingers and blew the kiss toward him as she opened the back door and headed out to her truck.

John rested his hands on the counter and lowered his head. No, she never would have left him—ever.

Abigail would have had dinner on the table, the house spotless, and Jacob would have been doing something—anything else other than kicking a ball into the walls. John would have come home and seen his wife rocking their baby, not his mother had that last pregnancy not gone so wrong.

He rubbed the stubble on his chin. She'd wanted three kids—he'd wanted four. Why couldn't they have known that the fourth would have cost her her life? Why didn't someone catch it earlier? Why had he pushed for it?

John fisted his hands and that was when he remembered the raw skin under the bandage.

He looked at his hand and the bandage—the bandage Kym had put there.

As quickly as he could he pulled the gauze from his skin. Kym. He was tired of thinking about Kym. She'd been the first woman since Abigail to make his blood warm and his pulse quicken. He'd walked with his head down for two years, but the day he'd run into her cart he'd looked up and there were those green eyes.

He threw the gauze into the trash. Why now? Why her? He didn't have time to think about women. He had four kids to tame and a business to run.

Just then Abby and Mason ran through the room and Cody began to cry from the play pen in the living room. There would be a day it would be all over and he was afraid he was going to miss it. But right now he was just too tired and all he wanted was a moment not to think about where the money for the new furnace they were going to need was going to come from. He didn't want to think about what third grade mess Jacob was in. And he certainly didn't want to think of Kym O'Bryne.

The noise in the basement has stopped and when John looked up at the back stair case there was Jacob.

"Hey, kid."

"Hey."

"How was school?" he asked, but he knew it was the wrong question to ask.

"Sucked. Carson is home schooled."

"Yeah, but his mom is home too."

He only nodded his head. "I know."

It was the sad face of his son that broke his heart the most.

"Heard you kicking the soccer ball around."

"Yeah. I'm bored. Carson has an Xbox too."

"There is always one friend that has more stuff, huh?"

Jacob nodded. "Can I go after school tomorrow and kick around the ball with him?"

"You need to get Abby home."

"She could come with."

That was quite a generous offer, he thought. "You'd take your sister?"

"Why not?"

That made John wonder what the ulterior motive was. But he didn't see any harm in it. He was always driving around town, he'd see them. The school and the fields were just across from the hardware store. Well, hell, he thought—the whole town was across from the hardware store.

"You'll keep an eye on her?"

"Yes."

"You'll be home by four?"

"Yes."

"Okay. I'll let grandma know."

Jacob gave him the slightest hint of a smile.

When the oven reached temperature, John pulled down the door and slid the pizzas onto the rack.

"Will you get your brother out of the play pen? I have to wash those other two monsters up and by then we can eat."

"Sure."

As Jacob passed by, John ran his hand over the top of his head. "Thanks, bud."

But Jacob said nothing. John knew he was tired of having any responsibility around the house and he wished he didn't have to ask, but that wasn't how it was at the Larson house. Four kids—one man. Life hadn't played fair and they were all paying the price.

***

Kym had bought half a dozen muffins at Malory's and a mint mocha coffee. As she looked around the bakery she saw that not much had been done on the renovation in the past two days.

"He'll be in later," Malory said with a grin curling up the corner of her mouth.

"Oh, Mr. Larson?" Kym asked as if she didn't know she'd been caught looking for him. "Your customers will have a reprieve from his cursing."

Malory chuckled. "His bark is much worse than his bite."

That's what had kept Kym up all of the night and had her mind elsewhere yesterday as well.

"I'm sure he's nice when you get to know him."

Malory nodded. "He's got it tough right now."

Before Kym could continue her investigation into the mysterious John Larson, the door to the bakery opened and a tall, handsome man with long dark hair walked in. The smile on Malory's face widened.

The man walked up to the counter, rested his elbow down and his chin in his palm. "Hey, Wil, someone knocked you up."

She laughed. "Yeah, only trouble walks in this town."

"I've heard that."

"So what do you want?" She'd inched in over the counter as much as her swollen belly would allow.

"I want you to close shop and let me show you what a real man is like."

She laughed easily and rested her hand on his cheek. "Damn, I thought I could forget all about you Christopher Douglas."

"Nah, I'm unforgettable."

Malory kissed him softly on the lips and then he turned his head and looked at Kym, who had been caught up in the banter between them.

"Ah," he said standing up straight. "I didn't notice you already had company."

Malory laughed again. "This is Kym O'Bryne. She owns the karate school."

"Oh, yeah." He held his hand out to her. "I'm the one who knocked up Wil."

Malory snorted. "That would be my husband."

Kym shook his hand. "It's nice to meet you." She looked him over. "Christopher Douglas. Hockey?"

"You know hockey?"

She nodded. "I have two older brothers." Kym could feel the heat from the cup she clenched in her hand. "I should go. I have lesson plans to finalize and classes starting at three. Thanks for the coffee."

"I'll see you soon," Malory gave her a wave.

"It was nice to meet you," she walked past Christopher who hurried to open the door for her.

"Likewise."

Kym walked out of the warm bakery and out to her car. When she looked back toward the building she could see Christopher walk behind the counter and lay his hands on Malory's stomach. He bent down and kissed the lump beneath her apron and lingered there as if he were talking to the baby. An ache moved through Kym's body. She'd never been in one place long enough in her life to find a man she could settle into such comfort with. What a wonderful thing it must be, to be loved like that.

She set her cup of coffee on the top of her car and pulled open the door. She set her bag of muffins on the passenger seat, retrieved the cup of coffee, and climbed in.

It took a moment for the heater to whirr up warm air, but when it did she backed out of the parking lot and headed toward the karate school.

She could hear the kids playing on the playground at the elementary school. It didn't matter what kind of mood she was in, children's laughter always made her feel better.

She figured that was why she enjoyed teaching. Though her teaching was strict, after class there was plenty of time for laughter and hugs.

Kym passed by the hardware store and caught a glimpse of John walking back into the building. Suddenly her heart rate kicked up. Why did he do that to her? He'd been nothing but crude when he was around her. She'd rather drop him to the ground in one fell swoop than to try to have a nice conversation with the man. But still, there was something about him which had kept her up for the past two nights.

She was just lonely, she decided. Malory was good for conversation, but besides her John was the only other person in Aspen Creek she had spent more than ten minutes with.

Seriously, she needed to get out and make more friends.

Maybe she'd start with Kelley Larson. That seemed reasonable enough.

She'd stop in there tomorrow. Surely she needed a key cut or some of those 3M hooks to hang up something at the school. No matter what, there would always be a reason to stop in at the hardware store. But she would absolutely make sure John wasn't there.

Chapter Four

Kym had exactly four students in her class at three o'clock. Their ages ranged from twelve down to six. It was hard to teach kids that varied in physical ability. But this was a white belt class and that meant everyone was at the beginning of their journey. The goal would be to have this small group of people eventually be her black belt class— she needed a black belt class.

They were learning basic moves. Front punch. Front punch. Turn and repeat. The twelve year old boy was doing it right and giving each punch his all. His six year old brother on the other hand seemed preoccupied with something outside.

Kym walked over to him and stood, her hands clasped behind her back.

"Mr. Pine, is there something better outside?"

The boy's eyes widened and his spine straightened. "No, ma'am."

"When we are in class we focus on our form, yes ma'am?" she added to force him to respond correctly.

"Yes, ma'am."

She gave him a curt nod and moved to the next student to help them. But it was then she noticed what had caught the attention of the six-year-old Pine boy. There was another set of eyes peering through the back door watching them.

"Now let's work on our back fist," she instructed as she backed off the floor and moved toward the door.

She quickly opened the door as two children began to run.

"Stop right there." Her tone was stern, but she hadn't raised the volume.

Both stopped and turned around. The older boy tucked the younger girl behind him.

"Are you here to take class?" Kym asked, again sternly.

"No. Just watching." The boy's voice shook as he spoke.

"Just watching? You don't get good at something by just watching."

The boy's eyes had grown wide and the girl peeked around him.

"What are your names?"

The children exchanged glances. "I'm Jacob. This is my sister Abby."

"And where are your parents?"

They exchanged looks again. "My dad is working. He said we could hang around after school."

This was where the town needed her. *Hang around.* That was what caused most problems in society, or at least that's how she saw it.

Kym crossed her arms over her chest. "My class is very small today. We could certainly use another young man and lady to join us."

Jacob shook his head. "We can't afford classes."

Kym gave him a nod. "Have you ever dumped a trash can or swept a floor?"

Jacob laughed and then straightened again and nodded. "Of course."

"Of course what?"

"Yeah, I've done that."

"The correct way to answer that is yes, ma'am."

The kids exchanged looks again and both answered at the same time, "Yes, ma'am."

She wanted to smile, but this was not the time or place. These kids needed her. They needed discipline.

"Come in. Take your shoes off and I will teach you how to bow onto the floor. We are working on basic moves today."

Both of them nodded and followed Kym into the school.

Within forty-five minutes she had seen a great change in the kids she'd pulled into the school. They followed along and answered commands correctly. This was what she was wanting for the community. A chance to make a difference.

When class was over and the other four students bowed off the floor, Kym walked over to Jacob and Abby.

"Did you enjoy the class?"

"Yes, ma'am," they both answered.

"Wonderful. Now, Jacob, the broom is in the corner by the bathroom. I'll need you to sweep up the mats. Abby, do you think you can handle the small trash cans in the bathroom and by the front door? They need to be dumped into the big can at the back door.

"Yes."

"Yes what?"

"Yes, ma'am."

This time Kym smiled. "Okay. Get to it and then you may go."

Both of the kids nodded and ran to do their jobs, bowing off the floor as the other students had done.

Kym walked to the counter at the front of the school and dug through the bin of belts she kept underneath. When she found two white belts that would fit the new students she set them on the counter.

A few minutes later Jacob and Abby came to her with their shoes and coats on.

"I have class tomorrow at three as well. Will you be here?"

A concerned look shifted between the two.

"I'd like to, ma'am. But our dad can't afford this."

Kym nodded slowly. "Do you think you could do another chore tomorrow to help me?"

"Yes, ma'am." The words were obviously coming easier now.

"I'd like to have you both in class tomorrow."

They nodded.

"I have something for you." She came around the counter with the belts in her hand. Both of the children's eyes grew wide.

Kym knelt on the floor. She held one belt in both hands and bowed to Abby as she handed her the belt and then repeated the move to Jacob.

He was smiling bigger than she'd seen any child smile.

"Thank you, ma'am."

"You're welcome. Bring them tomorrow and I will teach you how to tie them on."

They both smiled and nodded as they started for the door.

Kym stood up. "By the way. What is your last name?"

"Larson," Abby said quickly.

The name stabbed into Kym. "Larson? Are you Kelley's kids?"

Jacob stepped in front of his sister as if to keep her quiet. "No, ma'am. John is our father."

She felt as though someone had reached into her chest and squeezed her heart. "Oh." Her voice had dipped and she didn't like that.

"I'd like to talk to him about you training."

The kids exchanged concerned looks again. "I don't think he'd like that." Jacob looked away and then back at her. "Ma'am."

"Okay." She forced a smile on her face. "If you will help me out I will train you. Do we have a deal?"

Jacob nodded and smiled freely. "Thank you, ma'am."

He turned and all but pushed Abby out the door as they ran off.

Kym walked back around the counter and sat down in the chair. John Larson was married with children and the thought had never crossed her mind. She hated that she even cared. He was a horrible, cranky, mean man. But when she'd held his hand and wrapped it in gauze she hadn't felt that.

She was desperate to have something for herself. But it certainly wasn't John Larson.

Maybe she'd still make that friendship connection with Kelley. Kym still needed a friend and now they had Jacob and Abby in common.

As her next two students walked into the school, Kym stood up and smiled.

She had priorities now. Looking for a man was not one of them.

***

John paced his kitchen waiting for his son and daughter to walk through the door. It had been three days of staying after school to kick around a soccer ball—two days of them coming in later than the four o'clock they'd agreed on—and three days he hadn't seen them on the field as he drove by.

Jacob and Abby ran through the door and stopped immediately when they saw him standing there.

"It is four-ten."

"Yes, sir," Jacob said moving in front of Abby as he often did when he was about to take blame for something.

"We agreed you'd be home by four and this is the second day you've been late."

"I'm sorry, sir."

John moved toward him. "And what's with the 'yes, sir?' You sound guilty of something."

Jacob shook his head. "No, sir," his eyes widened when he said it. "I'm just being polite."

John looked at Abby who stood behind her brother with her eyes diverted. Oh these two were up to no good and he was going to catch them in the act.

"Go get cleaned up and we'll have dinner in a little bit. Jacob, get your homework started."

"Yes, si…dad," he said as he took Abby's hand and they ran down the hall.

John's mother poked her head around the corner of the kitchen with Cody balanced on her hip. "Why did you let him off the hook?"

"Because I'm going to let him lead me right to the trouble he's causing. I'm going to follow him right out of school on Monday and see where he goes."

"Why don't you trust him?"

"Did you see how he shielded her? She's keeping his secret."

His mother laughed, set Cody on the floor and watched as he toddled off. "John Larson, I remember you turning this town inside out when you were little. You and Chris Douglas and even Wil caused more trouble than that boy."

"Why do you think I intend to stop him? I know the possibilities."

She shook her head. "You turned out just fine. So will he."

Again, she blew him a kiss and let herself out the backdoor.

His mother was right. Chris and Wil came up with the best ideas when they were younger. But John was the one to carry out all the deeds. Oh, he'd had a switch to his rear more times than he could count. Then he thought about the time he'd punched Cade Carter right in the mouth because he'd made a move on his sister. Who would have thought the retired professional football player would end up teaching gym at the high school and marrying Olivia, the girl who had lived next door to Cade growing up?

The town was small enough that everyone was close to everyone else, even if they hadn't wanted to be. But there was still room for too much trouble. He didn't want that for Jacob. He already had enough to worry about. John would do everything he could to protect his sons and daughter. If that meant following him and reprimanding him in public to make a point, he'd do it.

Monday was going to be interesting.

Chapter Five

Kym tied on her belt and studied herself in the mirror. She was ten years old the day her grandfather tied her first black belt around her waist. A day didn't go by that she didn't wear the belt and think of the hard work she'd put into it. Martial arts wasn't just a sport—it was a way of life. As a teacher, she could share that with everyone—young and old. She had the honor of tying new black belts on children who had put eight hard years of work into it. She'd seen them sometimes transform from trouble maker into disciplined scholars and citizens. That was what she saw in Jacob Larson.

There was trouble in his eyes, the kind that would turn a good kid into a troubled teenager and a misplaced adult. He needed some confidence. He needed inner strength. And somewhere, he needed to learn peace.

What kind of father was John Larson if he didn't know where his son and daughter were everyday after school? How was it she ever felt anything for the man? First impressions were right. He was just a rude, crabby man. Well, she thought as she tucked her hair up in a tie, if she was going to make a difference in this town she'd start with Jacob Larson. Maybe she could help transform him into something better than what his father was.

Kym pushed back her shoulders and breathed in the calm that she would need for the next four hours. She'd heard the last school bell ring and soon her class would form. Today she was going to teach Jacob to jump and kick. She couldn't wait to see what he could do.

A few minutes later she saw the parking lot begin to fill with cars and Jacob and Abby were running across the field where other kids played. He held his sister's hand as they ran toward the school.

Kym stood near the door, her arms crossed over her chest. "Good afternoon, Jacob and Abby."

"Hello, Ms. O'Bryne."

"You'd better get changed. Class starts in a few minutes."

"Yes, ma'am."

She watched the two scurry off with the other students to take off their shoes and store their back packs. Her intention was to present them with uniforms if they kept training for the next few weeks, but for now she didn't mind them training in their school clothes.

John sat in his truck in the parking lot of the elementary school. Had his children just walked into Kym O'Bryne's school? What were they doing there? What did that woman offer them? He gripped his steering wheel tight. She could mess with him, but when she included his kids—she was playing with fire.

He drove from the elementary school, getting stopped at the one stop light on Main Street, and fought for street parking in front of O'Bryne's Karate School.

His jaw was tight and his hands balled into fists as he sat in his truck waiting to see if his kids would come out of the school. But they didn't. More kids went in and their parents seemed to be seated near the door. Well if his kids were in there watching they were about to find out he didn't like them there. John Larson wasn't one to be lied to.

He climbed out of his truck, the ground below him hard and slick. Slamming the door he headed to the entrance.

There were about ten adults standing between him and the floor he'd watched her work on. The very floor he'd had to kick his shoes off to walk across.

She was there in her uniform and her hair pulled back. He didn't like that seeing her made his whole body warm— with anger he was sure—maybe. John slid through the door and stood behind a woman who had been into the store a few times. She stepped over to make room for him without looking at him.

When he saw his children on the floor with white belts tied around their waist his vision actually blurred. He was so mad he could jump the two rows of folding chairs and have them out of there in ten seconds.

Jacob stood in line, his sister to his side, and they bowed when Kym spoke to them. The entire class did. Then she gave them all a command and they stepped back with their right foot and their hands came up in a guard. Kym adjusted Abby's hands and then began to count. With each number the students kicked in the air. Abby wobbled from side to side, but Jacob was strong. They yelled something with each kick and he could hear his son's voice above all the others, even the older students and the one dad who was out there.

As each minute passed, his son and daughter moved from one move to another. Their faces were serious. Sweat dripped from Jacob's hair. But there was a smile in his eyes.

John felt the pang of regret creeping into his gut. A smile behind blue eyes meant money and he didn't have any.

Kym looked up from her students for the first time and he caught her eyes. She'd smiled briefly until she obviously saw the narrow gaze he'd laid upon her.

She passed off the class to a teenager with a black belt, whom John recognized from town, and she headed toward him.

"I see you came to check in on your children."

He took in a chest full of air wanting to give her a piece of his mind. So many things whirled around in his head as he looked down at her and she looked back at him with those green eyes. Oh, he was going to tell her how it was. This was crap—his kids hanging out with her and lying to him. He wasn't going to have it, but the words weren't coming.

Kym touched his arm and that huge breath he'd sucked in stuck in his lungs.

"Look," she said just as Jacob jumped in the air lifting his right leg and then switched his left leg out and kicked the pad the teenager was holding. "He's a natural."

Yes he was.

But that had done it. He looked down at her. "They don't have my permission to be here."

She nodded as though she knew that. That infuriated him even more.

"Mr. Larson, why don't we step into my office and discuss this." She smiled.

"I don't think I need to."

But she touched him again. "Yes. Yes you do." She began to walk away from him and, as if he were under some spell, he followed.

John Larson walked through the door of her small office where she talked to parents and signed students up for classes. He was a big man. Though he hadn't had to duck to get through the door his head nearly grazed it.

"Please have a seat," she offered as she sat behind her desk.

He looked around for a moment and then back out the small window where he could see his daughter try the same move her brother had tried before, but she fell.

On instinct he moved to the door, but when she jumped back up and got in line to do it all over again, he stopped.

"Listen, Ms. O'Bryne, I didn't agree to them being part of all of this."

"I know. They said I shouldn't discuss this with you."

"They what?" He moved to the desk and rested his large hands on it. "You knew my kids were lying to me?"

She stood and met him eye to eye as he leaned over her desk. "I knew that you were too busy working to wonder where they spent their time after school. They chose to spend it here."

"They told me they were playing soccer."

"They've been learning martial arts, sir. And they are doing a dang good job of it too."

He stood up and crossed his arms over his chest. "I'm not paying for this. I didn't agree to any contracts or anything."

"I never asked you to pay."

He moved his hands to his waist. "You expect me to believe you'd just give them lessons?"

Kym stood straight. "Yes."

"I don't believe you."

"Sir, I don't lie."

"And what is with all the sirs?" He sat in the chair in front of her desk as if he no longer had the energy to stand any longer. "All week it has been yes sir, no sir."

She smiled. "Then they are learning discipline."

"By saying that—that's discipline?"

"It's one step."

She sat down behind her desk again and rested her hands, her fingers laced, atop it.

"Jacob is a fine young man. He needs some structure."

"And your kind of structure costs lots of money."

"Again, I didn't ask you to pay for classes."

He ran his hand over his chin and she could hear the whiskers rub against his palm. "And why is that? I'm a business man. You can't expect to make a living giving away your service."

"Jacob and Abby both have been helping out to earn their classes."

"Abby is six. What could she possibly do around here?"

Kym worked very hard to keep the smile from forming. "She has cleaned bathrooms, dumped trash, swept the floor, straightened chairs—shall I go on?"

"And that's good enough for them to take a class?"

"It seems to be amicable."

John ran his hand over the back of his neck. "Jacob has done his homework every night this week."

Now she smiled. "And when he's turned in his perfect assignments to me to look at he's received a stripe on his belt."

He sat silent for a moment. The anger in his eyes had diffused.

"Listen, I don't want to owe you anything. And them doing odd chores for you…"

"Those odd chores were our agreement."

He nodded. "You're sure about this? You're not going to change your mind next week and tell me I owe you thousands of dollars are you?"

"I don't do business like that, Mr. Larson."

"John," he said plainly.

"I enjoy your children. They are doing a wonderful job and I think Jacob needs this kind of structure."

John only nodded and that pleased her. It could have been one of those comments that caused him to come unglued.

"How many days a week are we talking?"

Kym folded her hands in her lap. "This particular class is everyday at this time, except Wednesdays. They are welcome to attend all of them. I ask that they attend two."

He nodded slowly as if he were thinking. "That would help my mother out if she only had the two in the afternoon until I got home."

"The two what?" she asked.

John looked up at her. "The other two kids."

Kym felt that same disappointment she had the first time when she found out John Larson had children. Now he had four. But then the thought humored her again. She didn't even like the man, so to be disappointed that he was married with four children shouldn't concern her.

She cleared her throat. "How old are your other two?"

"Four and two," he said flatly as though it was an automatic response and he was still thinking. "I'm going to talk to the kids about your arrangement. Them doing some manual labor is good for them. They need to learn to work for what they want."

"I agree."

"But it isn't enough. I noticed the front door doesn't quite swing right. It could use an adjustment. And the parking lot is a mess. If you had it lined then Mrs. Cavanaugh wouldn't take up half of it with that stupid Cadillac."

She held in the laugh. She'd meant to talk to the woman about that.

"The panels in the ceiling need replaced and come spring you could use a coat of paint outside."

Kym narrowed her gaze on John. "Are you trying to sell me items from the hardware store?"

His eyes changed now. He wasn't thinking anymore. "No. I was thinking those are things I could do for you to help cover the expenses of my kids spending time here."

She felt her mouth drop open and only an exasperated vowel sound emerged.

"Hey, unless them dumping your trash is enough."

"Mr. Larson..." He shook his head. "John, that is very generous of you."

"I didn't give you enough credit. I see what this has done for Jacob in the last week. Something tells me you have a lot more you could teach him."

"I'd like the chance to."

"Then I'll come by this week and fix your door." He stood from his chair.

Kym followed and moved to the door. She reached out and touched his arm. "Thank you for trusting me with your children."

John looked out the window over the floor where his children bowed to the instructor and class was then over. "They need to trust someone and you seem to fit that bill." He looked down at her. "All I ask is you don't disappoint them."

He opened the office door and walked out among the other parents.

Kym stood back and let the disappointment wash over her. He didn't trust her completely and that hurt her. She'd never do anything to upset a child—especially John's children. Jacob, especially, had a gift.

This wasn't something new. She'd had to prove herself to everyone her entire life. There would be a day John Larson understood her and when he did she'd be paid in full.

Chapter Six

It was well past seven when Kym's last student left. She could smell her grandfather's cooking and she knew she needed to get upstairs before something caught fire. He was still her job too.

"Ah, my Kym." He smiled as she walked through the door. "Dinner is ready."

"Grandfather, you should have let me…"

He held up a hand to stop her. He didn't like when she fussed over him so she stopped.

Her grandfather motioned to the bowl on the table. Inside was kimchi and rice—his most favorite comfort food. Usually this meant he was missing home. Kym understood, though it wasn't a place she missed—she missed her family.

The thought made her think about John Larson and his four children. It was probably dinner time for them too. Did his wife prepare him a grand meal every night? Did Jacob fuss over the tiniest thing? Did Abby eat peas? What were the other children's names?

"You're thinking too much. Eat," her grandfather nodded to her bowl.

She picked up her chopsticks and took her first bite. No matter how old her grandfather was, he had a way with kimchi and rice.

John took the bowl out of the microwave and set it on the table. Mason leaned in over the table and crinkled up his nose.

"Peas? I don't like peas."

"You're going to have six of them at least," John told him.

"Uh-uh." He sat back down and crossed his arms over his chest.

"No thank you taste or straight to bed."

Mason puckered up his lips. "You can't make me."

"Mason," Jacob said softly. "I'm going to eat my peas."

John gave Jacob a glance. *Really?*

"You don't like peas either," Mason quickly retorted.

"I'm going to try them again. I'll take my taste at the same time if you want."

John watched the exchange between his sons.

"O-kay," Mason said slowly.

John spooned a few on each of their plates and watched as they both skillfully balanced two peas on their forks.

"Ready? One, two, three," Jacob counted off and both boys ate a few peas.

John figured that was good enough for him. He wasn't a huge fan of peas either, but he couldn't waste the can. A moment later Abby ate a few peas and so did Cody—and no one was spitting them back up.

John realized they were all looking at him now.

"What?"

"Eat your peas, Daddy." Mason insisted and Jacob lowered his head grinning.

John looked around at the three other three sets of eyes watching in anticipation. He took a fork full and put it into his mouth. The peas squished between his teeth and the residue of them stuck to his tongue. He swallowed quickly. He still didn't like peas, but the three youngest kids at the table were cheering and they ate more.

Jacob looked up, still smiling, and began to eat his chicken.

When dinner was done John turned on the TV for the younger kids, as was routine, so that he could clean up without any interruption.

When he returned to the kitchen Jacob had already cleared the table and had the water running in the sink to fill it.

"What did you do with my son?" John laughed as he watched Jacob open the door to the refrigerator and put away the butter and the milk.

"I'm just helping out, Dad. Don't freak out."

"It's just that I've never seen you in here doing this before without making loud stomping noises with your feet and grunting every time you picked something up."

Jacob returned to the table and began to scrape the plates onto one plate and then stack the empties.

"Dad, why don't you go watch TV with them tonight. You should have a night off too. Most men aren't in their kitchens cleaning dishes before they give their kids baths."

John watched him. Eight. This kid was eight. What were eight-year-olds supposed to do? Help with the dishes. Takeover—not so much.

But Jacob seemed happy doing what he was doing and he wasn't complaining.

"So you really like doing karate?"

That made Jacob stop as he walked across the kitchen with his hands full of dishes.

"Yes, sir."

John should have expected the proper answer, but there was still some getting used to it.

"Ms. O'Bryne agreed to let you guys continue to help around the school."

Jacob set the dishes in the sink and turned off the water, but he didn't turn around.

"Dad, I'm sorry I lied to you about going to the school. I know we can't afford for us to do sports and clubs. But I really enjoy this. So whatever I have to do…"

John walked up behind his son and placed his hand on his shoulder. "It's not always going to be this hard, kiddo."

Jacob nodded, but John knew he was battling the tears, he too was fighting off.

"I miss Mom. But when I'm at the karate school I can make that all go away because I feel strong there."

"You look strong too."

Jacob turned his head and looked up at John. His eyes shimmered with the tears that didn't fall.

"I did?"

"You did." He smiled thinking about how proud Kym was of him too. It had shown in her eyes—those green, piercing eyes.

John kissed the top of his head and gave him a pat on the back. "I'll let you finish this and I'll go get their bath ready. Maybe we can all make it to bed before ten tonight."

He turned to leave the kitchen, but turned around to watch his son.

John had worried that losing his mother at six was going to ruin Jacob. A single man with four little kids—he was bound to ruin one of them. But even at eight, Jacob seemed to have found his path, at least for now. John would help keep him training if it was what Jacob wanted. And he couldn't deny having a little help around the house wasn't so horrible.

With Jacob's help, they were all in bed by nine—including John. He almost couldn't believe he was lying in his bed—the house silent—and he was alone in his room.

Jacob had read Cody a book while John finished giving Mason a bath. By the time John went back to put Cody to bed, he'd been tucked in tight and was already asleep.

Mason had been playing quietly with his Batman figure when John turned off his light and Abby had given him the biggest hug before she snuggled in for the night with her aunt's old American Girl doll.

Jacob took a few minutes to look over his homework before he hugged and kissed his father goodnight—which he'd stopped doing some time ago.

And now John lay in bed enveloped by dark and silence. The perfect opportunity for his mind to wander—and it wandered right to Kym.

That school didn't have a lot of students, but she was willing to train his kids for free. Why? He'd never been nice to her—or anyone. That's why it was so surprising that she'd take that on. After all, they had to have told her he was their father; she hadn't been surprised when he'd walked in.

Then again, maybe it was because he was their father that she wanted to do this for them. Maybe she thought she could change the next generation of Larsons since he was so socially inept.

But that would mean Kym O'Bryne had ulterior motives and John didn't think she had it in her. She was just a good-hearted woman—even he could see that.

John tossed and turned until he found a comfortable position in the old mattress and then he pounded his pillow into the right shape.

Since Abigail had died, John had never thought of another woman. He hadn't gone out on a date. He hadn't spent more than an hour with anyone but his mother, sister, and Wil. But now there was Kym and something about her had him thinking about her too often.

She was small—oh so small, but there was a strength that resonated from her. The posture in which she carried herself would make any six-foot man take a step back.

The way she looked at him with his wrench in her hand as he slid down the ladder the other day still burned in him. He could have killed her—or given her a huge bump on the head. But she was quick, prepared, and humored by his clumsiness.

He rolled over onto his side and punched his pillow again. He didn't want to think about Kym O'Bryne. She had to be years younger than him and he came with too much baggage. No one in their right mind wanted a grumpy old man, who was only in his mid-thirties, with four kids. By the time Cody was old enough to move out John would be able to find a date on the old man's dating website.

The thought made him chuckle, but then he flipped onto his back and laced his hands under his head.

There was something different about Kym O'Bryne.

He untucked one hand from under his head and ran it over his face. Tomorrow he would finish up the work at Wil's bakery. Maybe, just maybe, Wil would have a pearl of wisdom for her old friend. She'd tell it to him straight. He knew that when Wil was done with him he'd never think about Kym O'Bryne again. But as he closed his eyes and tried to sleep she was all he could think about.

Chapter Seven

Kym waited in line at Malory's bakery. She watched as the woman served up doughnuts and coffee with a smile all the while looking horribly miserable.

"Good morning, Kym."

"Good morning, Malory. How do you do this every day? You look uncomfortable."

Malory laughed as she rested her hands on the counter. "It's becoming a challenge, but I'll make it. At least the morning sickness went away months ago. Christopher had to help me back then. I couldn't stand the smell of anything baking."

Kym laughed. "If ever I can be of help in the mornings just ask."

"Be careful what you say. You never know when I just might need you."

Kym watched as she placed the muffins she'd ordered in a bag and poured her a cup of cinnamon coffee.

"This'll keep you warm," she said as she handed Kym her order. "I hear we're due to get some snow."

"I guess I'd better get prepared for that. Snow means a messy school."

She gave Malory a smile and turned to leave just as the door opened.

Kym knew it was John before she even saw him. It was early so his cologne was fresh and crisp. And again it was early enough that the scowl on his face was fresh too.

He held the door open for her and she ignored her rapidly beating heart and forced a smile and the married man with four children who frowned. "Good morning, John."

"Mornin'," he bit back as she passed by.

"The bakery looks nice. You've done a good job."

The compliment must have confused him because his brows knit, then he nodded.

"Thanks."

"Will I see Jacob and Abby today?"

"Yeah." He looked toward Malory who was signaling for him to close the door, so he did and she was more than surprised to find she was on the outside of the building and so was he. "If it ain't too much trouble I'll come by before they're done and check your filters on your furnace."

"That wasn't part of your list from last night."

"No, but snow is coming and you need to make sure the kids, and yourself, are comfortable. You can't afford for the furnace to go down."

"Right." She wanted to smile. Oh, she wanted to smile so much. "Jacob will enjoy having you there to see him."

He stuck his hand in the pockets of his brown Carhartt jacket. "He's really happy working with you. And if it keeps him from getting into trouble and doing his school work," he stopped and laughed, "and reading to his little brother after he washes dinner dishes, then I support you."

Kym batted her eyes quickly hoping the dampness would freeze up before the tears of pride spilled down her cheeks.

"He's helping at home?"

"More than you could know."

"I'll make sure he's rewarded for his hard work. So far he has the most stripes in the class, and it's only been a week. At graduation he'll be earning a medal."

"He'd like that."

Kym had an awkward way around this grumpy man. "My grandfather is waiting for his muffin."

John nodded. "Hey, tell him thanks for teaching my dad those relaxation methods. His doctor says he looks healthier than he has a in a long time."

Kym wasn't sure what he was talking about, but she was starting to feel the chill all the way to her bones, so she nodded and walked to her car.

She pulled open the door with her free finger and balanced her coffee and the bag into the car as she slid in behind the steering wheel. When she looked back at the bakery John still stood outside watching her.

She felt her breath stick in her lungs. With a wave she started the car and backed out of the parking lot, aware that he was still watching her.

There were a lot of things she wouldn't do and get involved with a married man was one of them. He was completely off limits, but her body didn't seem to understand that.

Malory was laughing when John pushed open the door. Christopher was standing behind her, a cup of coffee in his hand. He hadn't even seen him walk in.

"Dude, you're toast." Chris smiled behind his mug.

"And what does that mean?" John pulled his gloves off and shoved them into his pockets.

"The karate woman. You have eyes for her."

"Shut up." He ripped off his coat and hung it on the back of an empty chair. "She's teaching Jacob and Abby."

Chris's expression changed. "You can't afford two kids in karate."

"I know that. They worked it out with her. They're doing work for her in return for classes."

Malory smiled as she poured a mug of coffee and waddled around the counter to hand it to John. "I think that is very nice."

"I'm going to head over today and check out the building. It's old and could use a few repairs."

That sent Chris into a bout of laughter again as he walked around the counter and sat down at the table where John had hung his coat.

"The kids pimped you out?"

John narrowed his gaze at his old friend. "No. I offered."

"And you don't think you're toast?"

John picked up the coffee mug and sipped. He looked down where Chris sat, grinning up at him. He didn't like that anyone noticed. Yeah, he knew he was toast.

John spent a few hours working at Malory's. He was almost done, but he didn't want to paint until she wasn't around. Then he headed over to Maggie's restaurant to fix the garbage disposal. Thankfully she served him lunch. A trip by the store to see what else his sister had for him and he'd be on his way to Kym's to fix anything he could find to fix.

When he walked through the front door of the store he hadn't expected Cody and Mason to be there running to greet him. He quickly bent to meet them, as Mason had become crotch-high and had run toward him with full intent to hug him only to have him barreled over more than once.

"What are you two doing here?" He asked, but the both fought for him to pick them up, which he did. "Kelley, where's Mom?"

His sister just smiled. "Mr. Kym is giving some kind of meditation class over at the senior center and they both wanted to go."

"Is that so?"

"Uh-huh." She reached for Cody and pulled him off of John and held him on her hip. "Dad's doing really well with all the things he's learning. So she wanted to learn some new stuff too." She rubbed noses against her nephew and Cody laughed before resting his head on her shoulder.

"I wish I would have known she was going to do that. This isn't the safest place for these guys."

Kelley scoffed. "We didn't have any options growing up and we turned out just fine. Give them a break. You can't protect them every minute of the day."

"Yes I can. That's my job."

She shook her head. "You worry too much. If you don't stop you'll end up like dad."

He certainly didn't want that. The last thing he wanted was his kids orphaned and his sister left to raise them.

"Is she coming back before school is out?"

Kelley shrugged. "She didn't say."

John looked at the clock on the wall behind his sister. School would be out in twenty more minutes. He walked away, Mason still on his hip. Just like a customer in his own store he looked at all the filters for furnaces he had in stock.

Biting down on his lip he tried to remember what kind of model furnace was in Kym's building. He reached and grabbed two different sized filters for good measure.

"Write these down." He walked back toward the counter holding the filters.

"What are you doing with those?"

"Paying off my kids' karate classes."

Kelley grinned wide. "No kidding?"

"Listen, just do it."

Kelley set Cody down on the floor and he migrated to John's leg. She took out a notebook and wrote down the code for the filters.

"I didn't know the kids were doing karate," she said as she put the notebook back under the counter.

"I didn't either. Seems like they worked it out themselves with Kym."

"Kym?" Her smiled had grown even wider.

"That's her name."

"I know her name. I've met her. She's cute."

"So?"

"So!" Now Kelley was laughing just as Christopher had been. "You're still here, John. You're a living, breathing man. It's okay to enjoy a woman."

"She doesn't even like me."

"Not too many people do. You're a crabby old man, and I don't think you're all that old."

Didn't he know it? His disposition had never been good, but once Abigail had died he'd become, like she said, a crabby old man.

"I'm not looking for a woman. I have my hands full."

"I'm just saying maybe you could feel it out. I'd be happy to watch these guys if you wanted to take her out to dinner or something."

His sister's smile had pursed and now she was planning.

"No. No dinner. No dates. No dating," he said sternly. "Listen, I want to get these over there. Are they okay here with you?" He nodded to the two boys. One was playing peek-a-boo around his leg with the other which he still held on his hip.

"Nope. My busiest time is right after school. You know that. Mom said watch them until you got here and here you are."

John growled. "Where's their stuff?"

With his two bundled munchkins in tow, John parked in the parking lot at Kym's school, which was already dusting over with the few snowflakes which had begun to fall. He wanted to get it lined for her, but that would have to wait. Once the snow fell in Aspen Creek—it stayed on the ground.

John jump out of his truck, shut the door, and hurried to the other side to unbuckle the boys.

"You stand right here. Don't move," he told them as he walked to the back of the truck to grab the filters. When he came back around to the front the boys were gone. He looked toward the building and there they were, their little runny noses pressed to the window of the school.

He walked toward them and then noticed what had caught their attention.

Kym was in the center of the floor, her uniform on and her hair tied back. There was some kind of contraption in front of her with boards on it. It looked to be about four boards. She looked at them. Held her hand out as if to measure her distance, and then turned her back to the machine.

She took three very long and calculated steps away, then turned.

Her hands came up in defense. Suddenly her body seemed light as she bounced on the balls of her feet.

Then even through the glass on the front of the building and the wind in his ears, he heard her let out what he assumed was a battle cry and run at the boards.

In a fluid motion she jumped, one leg tucked up in front of her, the other leg extended out to the side. She flew through the air and right though those four boards which the contraption held.

"Cool!" both boys exclaimed in unison.

John felt the cold air fill his lungs as he'd gasped in. He's put his hand through a hollow door once and thought he was pretty cool. Nothing compared to what that woman could do to a helpless stack of wood. And his sister thought it would be wise to date her? Maybe Kelley had a death wish for him.

"I wanna do that," Mason turned to him and grinned.

"Me too. Me too," Cody chanted.

Wasn't going to happen, but they were making a lot of noise about it.

"Boys." He held up his hand to quiet them. "I have to go inside and fix something for Miss O'Bryne. You need to be quiet."

Mason nodded and Cody followed suit taking his father's extended hand. John motioned to Mason to open the door for them and he did, and then stepped behind his father who caught the door with his foot.

Kym turned around as they walked in and her eyes widened.

"You brought a crew with you," she said as she backed off the floor, bowing, before she turned and walked toward them. "Who are these guys?"

"This is Mason. And this one," he ran his hand over the thick blonde hair of his youngest son, "is Cody."

Kim squatted down so that she was eye to eye with Mason. "It sure is nice to meet you, Mason."

Mason took a step backward toward John's leg, but Kym didn't move. "It looks like your dad is here to put new filters in the furnace. Would you boys like to kick some pads with me?"

Mason was quick to nod.

"You don't have to entertain them. You have a class soon."

Kym looked up at him and smiled. "You're right. I do. And these two would be more than welcome to join us for a few minutes."

She twisted and looked at Cody. Her eyes softened. "Cody, would you like to join me? Yes, ma'am?"

John watched his son process the fact that the woman hadn't given him a choice. He nodded automatically even though he didn't move toward her quickly.

Kym smiled wider as she stood. "Looks like we are settled then." She held her hands out for each boy to take and John was surprised when both of them took her hands and walked with her toward the training floor. He couldn't hear her words, but he knew she was explaining the process to them as they all three bowed.

He wasn't sure he liked the fact that the woman had some ancient Asian magic she used on them. The commands, the bowing, the getting exactly what she wanted when she wanted it—that bothered him. Already his two oldest were working for her to take her classes. And now his two youngest were out there following every word she said to them. They didn't listen to him like that. And, as he walked to the back of the school with filters tucked under his arm, he realized he too had fallen victim to her voodoo with those green eyes.

John gritted his teeth as he made his way to the furnace. Oh, he'd gotten himself into this one. Who was he to offer help out of nowhere? That wasn't his style. And as he pulled up the door to replace the filter he realized that was just what he'd done. He'd been the one to volunteer. In fact, hadn't the woman said she didn't need his help?

And what was all that crap Chris was talking about him being toast? Stupid friends. They didn't know everything.

John examined the two filters. He took the one that wouldn't fit and set it against the wall. Then he slid the correct filter into the slot and looked around the back room of the school. The water heater was old. She was going to have to replace that soon, he thought. He'd have Kelley order one up and have it on hand.

He looked at the old windows. They'd been painted shut about a million times. That was a fire code violation. Oh Marcus Hunt would have a hay day with that.

He could hear Cody's little voice attempt at making some loud grunt as he kicked a pad and Kym cheered him on. Well if she wanted to babysit them for a few minutes he'd let her. No skin off his nose.

He noticed a screwdriver on the counter and he took it to the window. He could at least break some of the paint seal and see how much damage there was. And why not? She was entertaining the troops. She deserved this. John chuckled to himself as he drug the sharp edge of the screwdriver through the caked on paint. If she wanted to take on kids that weren't hers, then she should be stuck with them.

The screwdriver dug into the paint, but only managed to make a scratch.

He was going to need something much bigger than a screwdriver. Setting it on the windowsill he pulled a utility knife out of his pocket, opened it, and began making grooves into the paint. Now he was making progress.

Finally, the window had been freed from the captive paint. Wiggling the pane, he managed to get it to budge from the position in which it had been stuck in for years.

"I thought you were just changing out the filters." Kym's voice rang in his ears.

She stood in the doorway, her arms crossed over her chest and her head cocked to the side.

"Did that. Noticed your windows were sealed shut. That's a fire code violation. So I got one unstuck. It'll take some time to get the other four open."

Kym nodded slowly. "Cody and Mason did very well in class today."

John could feel the heat rise in his cheeks. Casually he looked at his watch. He'd been hiding in her back room for over an hour.

"I lost track of time. I didn't mean to leave them."

"Didn't you? It seems to me like you're the kind of man who likes to make a point." She was walking closer to him and suddenly even he, a man who towered a good foot over her and probably outweighed her by eighty pounds, was afraid of her. "You think I'm some crack pot looking to steal people's money and brainwash their kids. But I'm not."

"Now, I didn't say…"

"You don't have to. I see how you look at me."

He was hoping he was looking at her like she was crazy, but he was desperately afraid that he might be gazing—lost in those green eyes.

"Listen, Miss O'Bryne, no matter what I think, my kids like you."

She was nearly toe to toe with him now. "So you *don't* like me?"

John bit down on the inside of his cheek. This was more than a little uncomfortable. "I don't think you want me to like you."

"What I want is your respect. I want you to understand I have a service to offer to this town."

"I'm sorry I lost track of time," he apologized and then he realized he had nothing to apologize for. She said the kids could stay, and after all he was helping, and…oh, hell, there were tears in her eyes. "Hey, I'll pay for the class the little boys took."

She turned from him and now she didn't seem so scary. "I shouldn't have yelled at you. I'm a little homesick and I'm finding that it's harder to belong to this little town than I thought it would be."

"Escaping it was harder than I thought it would be too."

He turned her toward him and she brushed away the tears that fell as quickly as she could. A small smile emerged and perhaps a hint of a chuckle at his joke. "In the few months that I've been here I've only made one friend and Malory has too much on her mind to worry about being my friend."

John's hands were still on her shoulders, only now she was facing him. The moment was a little more intimate than he'd have liked, but he couldn't let go of her.

"Wil is a good friend to have. But I don't think she's your only friend."

"My grandfather has made many friends. He's made a name for himself in the community. I am only some woman that people overlook."

"Not all of us." He'd inched in too close. His hands had slid from her shoulders to her biceps. Her lips had parted as she looked up at him.

The room had grown very warm. His large hands were trembling. Every ounce of him hated that he'd done nothing but think about this woman, but as his body began to bend in toward her, he knew in his heart that he'd die an old unhappy man if he didn't kiss her right now.

Her eyes were drifting closed as he inched in even closer.

"Miss O'Bryne, are you back here?" Jacob's voice rang out.

John quickly stepped away from her, his hand catching a sharp piece of paint as he backed up against the window. "Crap!" He looked down at the paint piece lodged in his hand.

"Hey, Dad." Jacob gave him a friendly wave. "Ouch, what'd you do?"

"Paint chip in my hand. This window was painted shut."

"That's a fire code violation," Jacob said and John nodded and laughed. He'd taught him well. "Oh, Miss O'Bryne, where is your vacuum? Abby is having the little boys help her sweep up the training floor and I thought I'd vacuum the office carpet and the mats in the waiting area."

Kym stepped forward and shifted her shoulders back. "It's in the office in the corner."

Jacob nodded and walked away. Kym stood with her back to John. "Is your hand okay?"

"Fine."

"Never embarrass me like that again."

"Never what?"

She spun around and those green eyes had lost any attractiveness to them. "You are a married man with four beautiful children. How dare you make a move on me."

John was sure the top of his head was going to blow right off. How dare he? How dare…oh, she'd been moving in for that kiss. And married? Well hell yeah he'd been married. That's where he got those lovely kids. John took a breath to argue with her, but she turned and left the room.

Oh, the woman infuriated him. To hell with the water heater. She could suffer when it rusted out the bottom and flooded the damn school. To hell with her and her misfit feelings.

John closed his utility knife and shoved it into his pocket. He walked to the back door, turned the lock and let himself out, slamming the door behind him. He'd walk around the damn school and wait for his kids out front. If she made him feel that unwelcome then he'd just stay away.

Chapter Eight

Kym had managed to avoid her grandfather all evening by training until after he'd gone to bed.

Now, trying to climb out of her car, she realized how much she'd trained. Her body was sore and the newly fallen snow had brought with it a bitter cold she'd long ago had forgotten existed, but she'd felt it blow in off the ocean during New York winters.

The sun was peeking over the mountain and the valley was filled with a magnificent orange glow. She'd hoped she wasn't too early for Malory, but looking at the parking lot there had been many customers already.

She opened the door of the bakery and the scents filled her nose. It was a happy place, she thought.

"Good morning, Kym." Malory smiled, but it was certainly forced.

"Good morning."

"You're earlier than usual."

"I was looking for some friendly conversation and was hoping you wouldn't be too busy."

Malory turned and reached for a mug up on a shelf. It wasn't a usual mug that she'd use for customers. She filled it with coffee and pushed it across the counter. "Let's sit. I'll have a small break in customers for a bit."

Kym took the mug and walked to the table. Malory carried with her a small plate of muffin pieces and a cup of water. She waddled more than usual today.

"Here, mismatched muffins." She set the plate between them and then managed to sit down. "There's always a few that break apart. That's what we eat for breakfast."

"Thank you," Kym said as she took a small piece of what looked like chocolate. "This is good. I may have to take a whole one back to grandfather."

"Maggie, my mother-in-law, said he came by her place yesterday and sat with the men and played chess. She usually has to kick them out of the restaurant when she closes. But she said your grandfather was very gracious. He thanked her, shook her hand, and left her a generous tip."

Kym felt her cheeks tighten from her wide smile. "That would be him. He doesn't take anyone or any moment for granted."

Malory winched and her hand came to her side.

Kym's reaction was to jump and help, but Malory's calmness over the situation had her easing back in her seat.

"Are you okay?"

"Contraction. I've had a few, but we're still a few weeks away."

"Is that normal?"

"So I've been told," Malory said as she reached for her class of water and took a sip through a straw. "Oh, Mr. Wills is here." She adjusted in her seat and winced again.

"I'll help him. You tell me what to do." Kym stood up and walked around the counter.

The cold air came in with Mr. Wills and Kym shivered.

"Hello, Mr. Wills," Malory said from her seat. "Did you order this cold?"

"Not me. If I could have a beach on the side of that lake that stayed eighty degrees all year long I'd have one."

Malory laughed easily at the elderly man. "Mr. Wills, this is Kym O'Bryne, she runs the karate school. She'll help you this morning."

"That's fine," he said with a smile and looked at Kym. "Your grandfather is Kym too?"

"Yes sir, Sung-ki Kym, but he finds that going by Kym is much easier for others."

"He's a fine man." He continued to give his order to Kym and she did her best to fill it with a little help from Malory.

But it didn't stop at Mr. Wills. The door continued to open and close for the next hour and Kym insisted that Malory, who was still winching from time to time, sit still and let her help.

"You're a life saver," Malory said as the door closed and for the first time since Kym had stood it hadn't opened again.

"Do you mind if I fill my mug again?"

"Please!" Malory shifted with another pain as Kym retrieved her mug and filled it. "So tell me about you and John Larson."

Kym kept her back to Malory and finished filling her mug. Why was she surprised she'd asked her about him? After all that was why she'd come so early in hopes of learning more about the man. She needed to let go the stupid notion of caring for him. Kym wasn't a home wrecker and she wasn't going to start either.

"Tell you what?" She finished pouring her coffee and walked back to the table without making eye contact with Malory.

"Has eyes for you, in case you didn't know that."

Kym picked up her mug and put it to her lips. How was it that this married "friend" of John's didn't seem to see a problem with the eyes he had for her?

"I think you're mistaken. We have a working relationship and that is all."

"Nah, I've known John my whole life and the only other woman he looked at like that was Abigail."

The coffee burned as it slid down her throat. Abigail. She assumed that Abby would have been named after her mother.

"Abigail is his wife?"

Malory nodded as she sipped from her water, but Kym found that unnerving. How could she sit and casually ask her about John and then discuss his wife with her?

"I've never met his wife," Kym said as she set her mug on the table and looked back up at Malory.

Malory's eyes had changed and she leaned in over the table as much as she could. "Met her? Why would you have met her?"

"John's wife? I haven't met many people. I haven't run into her yet." And now she feared doing so. If she knew what John had almost done last night—Kym was already mortified.

"Kym, Abigail died almost three years ago."

Suddenly the room grew frigid cold. How had he not mentioned that? "I didn't know."

"There were complications with her pregnancy. She went into labor with Cody and something went wrong."

Kym lifted her fingers to her mouth. "Oh."

"She'd only wanted three kids. John had wanted four. He holds himself responsible for her dying."

"Things like that just happen."

Malory rubbed her stomach. "I know."

"I'm sorry. It is very insensitive of me to talk about this with you. I'm sure you have your own worries about your baby."

Malory smiled. "I do, but I'm not worried that anything will happen to me. Abigail's situation was unique to her."

"No wonder he's so crabby."

Kym's comment had set Malory into a fit of laughter until a pain in her stomach drew her back. "He's a pain in the butt isn't he?" She let out a breath. "Can't help but adore him though. His children are wonderful. He's doing a good job with them."

"That's why Jacob is so protective over Abby."

Malory nodded. "He takes his role as big brother very seriously." Malory winced again. "Oh, speak of the devil himself."

Kym quickly turned in her chair and looked out the front window. John had driven up and parked his truck right next to Kym's car. He was loading up a bucket with tools and heading into the bakery.

This was the sign that Kym should leave.

She turned back to thank Malory for the coffee when she noticed her face was red and she was panting.

"Malory, what's wrong?"

The door opened and John stepped through. He took one look at Malory, dropped the bucket, and rushed over to her. "How far apart?"

"They just started moving in faster," Malory answered and let out a few controlled breaths.

John took his cell phone out of his pocket and hit a few buttons. "You're time is up buddy," he said as he helped Malory to her feet. "I'll meet you at the hospital. Wil is in labor."

He threw the phone down on the table and Kym disconnected the call. She sat helplessly as John swept Malory off her feet and started for the door.

"Get her coat," he called back to Kym.

There was a coat rack by the door and hanging on it was one coat with a purse tucked up under it. It had to be Malory's. She grabbed it and hurried out the door toward the truck.

John was already helping Malory into the seat when she reached them. He ripped the coat from her hands and covered Malory with it. Then he took the purse and tucked it at her feet.

Just as quickly, John shut the door and hurried to the other side of the truck.

Kym moved back to the building as John backed up and sped out of the parking lot.

She stood alone outside in the cold, her coat long forgotten inside, and tried to catch her breath.

So many things ran through her head. The pain in Malory's face was the first thing she thought about. She'd never been around a baby or even a pregnant woman, but John hadn't even given it another thought. He knew she needed him. He'd scooped Malory up as if she were a doll and carried her out to his truck. She couldn't even imagine what would have happened if Malory's labor had progressed further. Tears were freezing in her eyes. Kym realized she was good at taking kids and teaching them how to be ready for anything and yet she wasn't ready for anything. She wasn't ready to take care of Malory had she needed her. And she certainly hadn't been ready to deal with the crush her heart was going through. Pity had enveloped her when she'd learned about Abigail. John was a crushed man.

Her heart ached for him and even more now she'd wished he'd finished that kiss. But not having known then what she was faced with now, she would have probably come to her senses and dropped him to the ground.

No, she wouldn't have. She'd been paralyzed by his hands on her. His dark eyes had softened so that she had no defenses against them.

But now, now he'd seen her when she wasn't *ready for anything.* Oh, she'd been stupid to tell him that when he'd dropped that wrench. But he'd needed to be put in his place.

Kym bowed her head. Now she'd been put in hers.

When her limbs had gone numb from the cold she headed back inside. Someone would come to take over or lock up, she was sure. But she'd stay until they arrived.

A car started up the road toward the bakery. That moment made her realize that she was there to help now. She'd had enough practice during the morning rush, she could help anyone that came into the shop.

A few minutes later an enormous man climbed out of a mini-van and headed for the door. She wanted to laugh. Was it the water in the town that made the men here so gigantic?

"Oh, hey," he said as he let the door close behind him. He let the zipper down on his jacket a little and a tiny head peeked out. "Got damn cold out there this morning, didn't it?"

She wasn't sure if he was talking to her or the baby he'd bundled up in his jacket.

The man looked up at her. "You own the karate school don't you?"

She smiled. "Yes. I'm helping out this morning I guess. Malory went into labor."

The man's eyes grew wide. "No kidding." He laughed a deep laugh. "I'll have to give Chris hell now. Wait till that little guy pukes on him one time. Poor Wil. She'll have her hands full."

Kym now knew this man was an Aspen Creek native. Depending on what one called Malory it gave away the truth to whether you came from the town or were transplanted there.

The man balanced the infant against his shoulder and held out his hand to her. "I'm Cade Carter. My wife Olivia and I grew up with Chris and Wil."

"Cade Carter?" She shook his hand. "You played football."

He nodded. "That seems like a long time ago."

"My brothers watched you."

"You don't watch football?"

She shook her head. "I train too much to watch other sports."

"Too bad." He gave her his order and then bounced the baby on his shoulder as she retrieved his coffee. "So how's the school?"

"It's going well, thank you," she said as she put the lid on his coffee.

"I took a few lessons there when I was a kid and did some training in Wisconsin, but never really pursued martial arts."

Kym set the cup on the counter and went to wrap up his muffin. "It's hard getting it going again after most of the students left. But we will make it."

"You know, I teach gym over at the high school. I'll bet we could work you into the curriculum one week. The kids could learn some self-defense. They won't be in this town their whole life if they're lucky."

"I don't know."

"Really. We could do it on all levels. The schools are all in the same place. Why don't we talk about it? Maybe it'll help you get a few students and it'll be something useful for the kids to learn."

Kym smiled. "I'd like that."

She set his bag on the counter and gave him the total.

"Dang. Wallet's in the car." He lifted the baby off his chest and dangled him over the counter. "Here, hold him. I'll be right back," he said as she took the baby. As Cade opened the door John barreled through.

"Are you crazy leaving her with him? She doesn't have the first clue as to what to do," he snarled and proceeded to walk toward the area with the plastic sheeting and set down two cans of paint.

Cade laughed and continued out the door.

Kym, desperate to not look like an idiot, pulled the tiny boy to her chest and gently patted his back.

John walked up next to her and took the baby from her. "Hold his head. He's too little and you have to protect his head."

He held him in his enormous arms and rocked from side to side.

There was a side to this man that came out at the strangest of times. The door opened again and Cade walked back through.

"Leave my son with a pretty woman for one second and you steal him away."

John shifted his eyes at him and Cade offered a glance that begged for forgiveness.

Kym finished the sale and handed Cade back his change. John smiled at the baby one last time and handed him back to Cade.

"How is Olivia?" John asked

"Back to work. I'm headed in to town to take him for his checkup since my first class doesn't start until ten. Parker has been real nice about letting her take him in with her."

"He was always a decent guy," John added.

"Yeah. Hey give Wil my best if you see her. I'll try to stop by and visit when I know the baby is here."

"You won't be waiting long," John said as he headed toward the cans of paint. "Water broke before I got her to the hospital. Chris nearly passed out when he saw her. He's such a wimp."

Both men chuckled.

Cade balanced the baby tucked into his coat with one arm and his bag and cup in the other and walked out the door.

When the door shut the air grew thick. Kym was all aware that it was only her and John in Malory's bakery, only now she knew the truth behind John Larson.

"Are you going to paint now?" Her voice shook as she asked?

"I was only waiting on Wil to get out of here for a few days."

"Can I be of any help?"

He didn't look up at her. "You got a job to do right there for a few more hours. She called in the old owner who will help out for a bit after tomorrow. But for now she needs you right there. Unless you have other things to do." He never looked up from the paint can, which he'd opened and begun to stir.

"No. It's Wednesday. It's my day."

"Right. You'll want to go train or something."

Kym tightened her fists to her side. It was already eleven o'clock and Malory's bakery usually died down until after lunch. Her business was morning treats and bread on the way home. Lunch belonged to the diners in town.

She sucked in a few breaths of courage and walked toward the table she and Malory had occupied earlier. "Can I get you something to drink?"

"She doesn't carry anything I'd need at this moment."

The fury he caused in her was starting to erupt inside of her. "In other words you need something a little stronger than coffee to deal with me?"

That had his head shoot up. "I find it better to just avoid you all together. But since you're a healthy young woman, who isn't pregnant, I'm going to paint today so I'm done when Esther gets here tomorrow. She's about eighty and doesn't need this stuff being done around her either. As you can see, I'm on a deadline."

"Well, I certainly wouldn't want to bother you any more then."

She picked up the mug and the water glass from the table and started toward the kitchen. As she set them in the sink and turned around to retrieve the plate she nearly ran right into the wall that was John Larson standing right behind her.

"You want to know what a bother you are? You have my kids doing chores that I never could get them to do. You have this voodoo magic over everyone in this town and it has them doing things they wouldn't do."

"Such as?"

"Such as offering to fix crap."

"You offered that."

"I know I did. I don't do that."

"Well then I think you have the problem not me." She tried to go around him, but he shifted, cutting off her path.

"You are my problem." He stepped in closer to her just as he had last night. "You know damn good and well you were moving in to kiss me last night too."

"I shouldn't have."

"You say that because you were in a position of authority last night. I get that. But telling me not to embarrass you, that was crap."

"I'm sorry." Her stomach had turned over from the guilt of that moment, but mixed with the beating of her heart and the heat of her skin she wasn't so sure she wouldn't collapse on the floor. Would he catch her as he'd caught Malory, she wondered.

"Sorry for what? Almost kissing me or for making me feel horrible about wanting to kiss you?"

She could feel his breath on her cheek. His enormous body had moved in so close she was now pinned against the counter. Was he only making a point or had she been on his mind too?

"What is it?" His voice was deeper and airy. Her eyes had closed and she could feel her lungs working double time trying to keep breath in her.

She forced her eyes open. "I didn't want to be a home wrecker."

He stopped moving in to her and pulled back. His eyes were wide. John bit down on his lip and cleared his throat.

"Home wrecker?"

"I didn't know about Abigail until this morning."

He stepped back and rubbed his chin with his hand. "You didn't know I was some poor old widowed slob, huh?"

"I don't think of you like that."

"Right. I'm the nice guy who was sweeping you off your feet."

He was very good at this guilt thing. "You've been on my mind a lot. I was heartbroken when I found out Abby and Logan were your kids."

"I'm that bad huh?"

Kym stepped toward him and rested her hand on his arm. "No. I just figured I was too late."

John turned to her again and now was right in front of her. His enormous hands had come to her waist.

"Too late for what?"

He made her so nervous. If he were attacking her she could deal with it. But he was holding her. His large fingers played with the nerves on her hips. His chest was working as hard as hers to keep his breath moving. What did she have to lose at this point?

"Too late to fall for you."

"Fall for me?"

She couldn't say she loved him, that would make him run. She only nodded and a groan came from him as he moved her back to the counter.

"You hate me."

She shook her head. "I want to."

"I'm not very nice."

"You have reason, but I don't think you're too bad."

He'd pushed himself to her and now she felt every hard part of his body pressed against her.

Kym raised her hands to his chest as his head lowered to her ear.

"I have four kids."

"I know," she whispered as she closed her eyes and let the moment wash over her with his breath in her ear.

"They come first."

"They always should."

She felt him swallow hard and his fingertips began do dig into the flesh on her hips.

"I've been losing a lot of sleep over you." His breath was hot against her neck. "I take relationships very seriously."

Relationship. Was this what she wanted? She didn't know him—but she wanted to. She sucked in a deep breath. "So do I."

He pressed his body closer to her. "If I kiss you, it means your mine." He took a breath. "It means all my crazy life is intertwined with yours. It means…"

"It means I'm an adult and I know what I'm getting myself into," she said as she reached her arms around his neck and brought him to her mouth.

Kym's mouth was on his and her fingers were now in his hair. He moved one hand to the counter to brace himself as she slid her tongue past his lips and into this mouth.

John's head spun. It had been years since he'd kissed a woman and it hadn't quite had the same effect on him as it was right now. His mind was going a million different places. He thought he should stop her—he was a cranky old man.

Oh hell, maybe this was why. He'd needed more kisses.

He should stop her, because it was disrespectful to the memory of Abigail, but her teeth on his lips made him think otherwise. Abigail would want him to fall in love again.

Then there was just that…falling in love. Could he do that? Did he have it in him?

He pushed against her harder. His body was taking over.

Their breath was growing thick—together. Their hands were searching each other—together. Their lips, their tongues, their thoughts—were together.

It could have been only seconds or perhaps it had been minutes, but finally, out of breath, Kym collapsed against him resting her head to his chest.

He held her close. He didn't want to see disappointment in her eyes. He didn't want to face reality of what this meant—not just yet.

Chapter Nine

John had taken Kym up on her offer to help him paint Wil's remodeled area. It wasn't that he'd needed the help; he just wanted her near him.

They were nervous around each other. He'd asked her about her family and she'd gone into long detail about her Korean mother and her Irish father and her two brothers. He had to admit he was envious that she'd lived in so many places. And likewise she'd shared that she was envious that he had such stability having lived in the same town his whole life.

The call had come in from Chris just as they were finishing that he was the proud father of a baby girl.

John had laughed right out loud and said, "Well, my friend, girls play a mean game of hockey too. Your wife did just fine in net."

He'd noticed Kym grow quiet after that and he hadn't wanted to ask her why.

When they were done painting there was an awkward moment between them when neither of them knew what they were supposed to do next.

"Do you pick up the kids from school?"

He shook his head. "No. Usually I'm working so they walk home. Or go to your school."

"Right." She smiled and tucked a fallen piece of hair behind her ear. "I guess on Wednesdays they're all home waiting for you, huh?"

"Yeah." It was the most pathetic conversation they'd ever had. They were better off when they were yelling at each other.

"Grandfather and I eat dinner together on Wednesdays, though since he's become a regular at Maggie's he hasn't been hungry for dinner too often."

John had laughed at that. "She makes the best grub around. But from what I hear, your grandfather has made many friends around town. Even my mother told me yesterday that Mrs. Clemens was going to fix him dinner."

"He might have mentioned that," she said, but not as humored as he'd been by the thought.

They cleaned up the paint and after she'd closed for the day. Maggie showed up to clean up the bakery and get ready for the next day.

John offered to stay and help her, but Kym had taken the opportunity to duck out. He'd walked her to her car when Maggie had gone in back.

"I wonder if I should come by in the morning and help," she said as she ducked into her car, started the engine, and then came back out to talk to him.

"Esther, might protest."

"Oh," she said softly.

It was supposed to be a joke, but it hadn't worked that way.

John stepped in closer to her, lifted her chin with his finger which was nearly numb from the cold. "Will I see you tomorrow?"

The glimmer came back to her eyes. "I would really like that."

He knew what that was. She was afraid that now that he'd kissed her—or she'd kissed him—and he'd said all that stuff about her being his that he'd continue to be the grumpy old man she'd been putting up with the past few weeks.

John leaned in and gently kissed her soft, cold lips. They warmed under his.

She smiled as she pulled away and climbed back into her car and drove off.

He stood for a moment longer, until her car was out of sight, and then he went back into the warmth of the bakery.

Maggie was standing at the large sink, her back to the door, when he walked back inside.

"I didn't see that coming," she said as he took down the plastic tarp which had been keeping the refurbished area blocked off.

"What's that?" He rolled up the tarp and set it in his growing pile of supplies.

"You and Kym. I haven't heard any gossip about the two of you. I'm just a little surprised, that's all."

This was the part about small town he'd never cared about. Everyone was in your business. He wanted to get mad, maybe even give Maggie a piece of his mind—but she didn't work like that.

She had the influx of all the gossip in town. After all, she owned one of two of the diners in town. But she wasn't a gossip herself.

John continued to clean up, but Maggie stood and watched. That only meant she wasn't going to let him off the hook until he gave her some information.

"Why does it surprise you?"

"Just because I haven't seen you look at a woman since you swooned over Abigail."

"That was a long time ago. She's been gone a long time too."

"Not that long," Maggie added as she picked up a tray she'd washed and began to dry it off.

"How long do I wait? Cody is almost three. He's never had a woman in his life but my mother."

Maggie set the tray down and walked toward John. "Is that what you're thinking? That Kym O'Bryne would be a good replacement mother for your children?"

No, that hadn't been what he'd thought at all.

He ran his hands over his head. "Maggie, I don't know what I think. I've never looked at another woman. Abigail was everything to me. I convinced her to have another baby and I lost her."

"You can't keep that eating you up."

"Well, it does." He moved to the counter and leaned his hip against it. "I don't know what it was about Kym that made me want to be with her. And I was anything but nice to her."

Maggie smiled and rested her hand on his. "Honey, you've been less than nice to most people for years."

He grumbled.

She moved her hand and laughed.

"John, I'm just surprised. Not disappointed. She seems like a very nice lady."

"Right. So why does she like me?"

"Are you asking me for the answer or are you asking yourself?"

He wasn't even sure. So in his usual style, when things got too deep for him, he began to carry his tools to the door and then out to his truck. When he came back in for the last can of paint Maggie had put on her coat.

"I'm going to go see my new granddaughter," she said beaming with delight.

"I'll bet she's beautiful."

"Oh, and she has a head full of dark curls." She rested her hand on his shoulder. "Make sure you drop by and see her."

He nodded. "I will."

"I can't believe you all are grown up and have families of your own. I can honestly say that I never thought you or Chris would find women who would put up with you."

He bit down on his lip. Abigail wasn't just any girl back then. But she had loved him until the very end.

"We were a handful, huh?"

"You were, but you've grown into fine men." She moved in and kissed him on the cheek.

She locked the door to the bakery as John put the last of his tools in his truck. As Maggie drove away she waved back at him.

The cold was numbing his limbs, but there was an ache in the pit of his stomach. He didn't want to be someone to be put up with for the rest of his life. He didn't want his kids to think he was a harried, crabby old man.

And he didn't want Kym to think that either.

He quickly looked at his watch. It was nearing four o'clock.

And suddenly he remembered, he'd taken two furnace filters to Kym's last night. He'd left one in the back room when he stormed out.

His arms warmed up as they lifted up the tailgate of his truck. The truck might have been warm as he drove toward Kym's school, he wasn't sure. The heat from just the thought of her was keeping him warm.

As he cleared the bottom of the hill he could see the school. Her car was parked on the side of the building as it always was. She was there. The filter would be the perfect excuse to stop by. If there was any question about, it he could simply say he needed to get it back in stock.

Maybe she'd be down on the floor training and he could see her. All he wanted was to see her before he settled in for an entire night of homework, dinner, and baths.

Guilt burst through his warm thoughts. Homework, dinner, and baths were more important. He had to remember that. Even with Kym in his life he couldn't betray his children's stability.

Slowly he drove past the school. The lights were on and she was training, just as he thought she would be.

John forced himself to drive on and go home. The request had been for macaroni and cheese for dinner. Already he had heartburn.

Kym had seen the familiar truck pull through the intersection, slow down, and drive on. She saw a lot of things in that mirror and the man who had kissed her and told her that meant she was his, had just driven away in the opposite direction.

A tear fell down her cheek and she brushed it away as she pulled herself into a ready stance and began her form again.

She had no right to think he'd stop. He was very clear that his four children came before her and she'd said she understood that.

Her arms moved in a pattern that was all from memory and her mind continued to process everything she'd done in the past two days.

And what she'd done was fall in love with a man who didn't have time for her.

Kym missed a step which caused her foot to turn too much and her knee torqued the other direction. She went down quickly on her butt twisting her knee even further.

She winced from the pain and hugged her leg to her chest. The tears flowed now as much from the pain in her knee as from the pain in her heart.

The cold air from outside blew through the school as the door was pushed open and someone walked through.

"We don't have any classes tonight," she said trying to steady her voice and knowing she couldn't stand up to walk in that direction quite yet.

"I know. That's why I thought I'd stop and see if you'd like some very crappy macaroni and cheese for dinner."

His deep voice resonated in her ears and the tears kept falling. He'd come back. He'd turned around and came back.

A moment later she could see him at the edge of the mat taking off his boots and setting them to the side. For a moment he hesitated, bowed, and then walked toward her.

"Why are you sitting in the floor crying?" His voice had grown soft as he knelt down in front of her.

She shifted her gaze up to his. "Many reasons actually. But mostly because I've just twisted my knee and I can't get up yet."

John maneuvered until he was seated on the mat facing her. He touched her leg and then lifted the edge of her pant leg up until he could see her knee.

She couldn't protest. Not only did she enjoy feeling his hands on her skin, but that caretaker in him was back and he was very gentle.

"How far can you straighten it?"

"Not much further," she said wincing as she tried.

"You're already swelling. You need some ice." He worked his large fingers around the muscles of her knee and even under her pant leg up her thigh.

Kym nearly moaned at the intimacy in his touch, but then he hit a muscle that nearly sent her through the roof.

"Ow!"

"Sorry," he said, but he continued to massage her leg. "Now how far can you straighten?"

She was able to set it down further. "You're really good at that."

She watched his Adam's apple bob in his throat as he swallowed hard. "Abigail studied massage once. She'd wanted to be a physical therapist. Things changed, but she taught me a lot of things. I was always hurting myself."

Kym smiled. "So not much has changed?"

He laughed. "Not much."

His hand lingered on her thigh, just under the cloth of her uniform pants. As Kym caught his eye he began to pull back, but she caught his hand, kept it on her skin, and moved her body in closer to him.

He was searching her face with his eyes. Uncertainty had clouded his face, but she wasn't going to let that stop her. He'd come back for a reason and she had to assume the reason was that he was falling in love with her too.

Kym kept one hand on his, on her leg, and she brought the other to his neck.

"I saw you drive by earlier."

"I didn't want to complicate things with the kids," he said moving in closer to her.

"Me eating macaroni and cheese might do that."

His body shifted even closer to her. "It's the chance I'm ready to take."

At that moment his mouth came to hers and there was a fire lit behind his kiss.

His fingers tightened on her thigh and his other hand came to her cheek.

John's tongue explored her mouth, urgency groaned from his throat, and his hand sought to pull her closer—until she winced.

John pulled back. "I'm sorry. Did I hurt you?"

"No. I did. I can't get close enough to you."

He rested his forehead to hers. "I guess there is plenty of time to do this, huh? Though I think I might burst if I don't get a kiss that lasts more than a few minutes."

She wondered if he could sense that she felt the same way.

John pulled his hands back and got to his feet. "C'mon, let's get you on a chair and I'll get you some ice for your knee."

And just as he had with Malory, he scooped Kym up into his arms and carried her off the floor.

John wondered if she even weighed a hundred pounds. Honestly, when Abby was asleep and he carried her to bed, she weighed more than Kym did. But having her pressed up against him like she was, only made him want her even more.

This kind of need wasn't good for a person, was it?

John carried her to one of the chairs in the parents' waiting area and propped her other leg up on the other chair.

"Okay, where do I find an ice pack?"

"In the back room in the freezer."

He lingered there for a moment to look at her then went to retrieve the ice pack.

It was right where she said it would be and when he turned he saw the furnace filter he'd left there. John moved to grab it and then stopped. What would it hurt to come back tomorrow for it?

As he walked back to her he could hear a cell phone ringing, but he knew it wasn't his.

Kym sat up taller on the chair. "Will you reach that for me? My phone is on the counter."

John reached for it and handed it to her then went about putting the ice pack on her knee as she answered.

"Hello?" She said as he put the ice to her skin. She jumped and held in the laughter that followed. "Grandfather? Where are you? Oh, she did?" Kym was smiling wide. "It isn't any problem. Yes," she said and her eyes moved to his. "I have dinner plans."

There was a familiar squeezing of his heart when she said it—that familiar *can't get enough* pain that came with love.

"I will see you later, Grandfather. Enjoy your dinner."

She pressed the button to end the conversation and kept her eyes locked on John's.

"Will you help me to my car? It seems as though my grandfather is too busy to dine with me."

He smiled. He wished he could just take her home and not worry about where they ended after dinner, but he knew she understood.

"Do you want to change?"

This time he watched her as she swallowed hard and her lips parted. "I'm very afraid that if I even thought about taking my clothes off right now things might end very differently."

Every muscle in his body ached and he tightened his hands into fists. "Your choice," he said a bit too airy.

"My clothes and my keys are in my office. Maybe if you help me over there I can get changed and you can go warm up my car."

John nodded. "I think that might be the safest plan."

As he helped her to her feet he also thought that maybe safe wasn't the way to play this at all.

Chapter Ten

John watched Kym limp out of the school. She needed to wrap that knee, but he was sure she knew that. Maybe he had something at home to take care of that. After all, he did have all of Abigail's supplies.

Kym stood at the door and locked it. John hurried to her side, bent down, and wrapped his arm around her waist to help her to her car.

"This is horrible," she said. "Maybe I'd better take a rain check on dinner."

"Nope. I'll carry you home if I have to. You have me all worked up. I need more than a few minutes with you."

As they reached her car he let her stand on her own.

"I do feel the need to warn you," he said. "This will be like no date you've ever been on."

Kym laughed. "I've met all your children. I'm sure I will be fine."

"Okay," he said pulling open her car door. "Don't say I didn't warn you."

She had laughed off his warning, he thought as she followed him through the streets of Aspen Creek to his very meager home. And she was probably right. She had a way with his kids that even he didn't. But it had slipped his mind that his mother would be there.

As he pulled into the driveway next to his mother's car he wondered just what kind of headache bringing Kym home with him was going to cause him. His mother was known to be a bit of a gossip, but would she really do that to her own son? Yes.

He let out a breath. Well, if he was going to make Kym part of his life it started right now.

Kym parked her car on the street and took a deep breath to calm her nerves. John was bringing her home for dinner. That was an enormous step. What if the kids didn't want her around? Would it be too awkward to have their karate instructor in their house? Maybe she should just tell him she didn't feel well. Her knee hurt. Her stomach hurt. Her...

He knocked on her window and she jumped in her seat. Now her back hurt.

John opened the door. "You didn't look like you were even going to try to get out of the car."

She mustered a smile. "I'm nervous."

"You've met my kids, remember?"

This was going to be okay she convinced herself as he took her hand and helped her out.

"How's your knee?"

"Twice the size it was."

"C'mon. Let's get you inside and get ice on it. You should elevate it and I'll wrap it too."

She limped away from the car and John shut the door. "Are you going to be sending me a bill later too?"

"On your next injury. This one is on the house."

She turned and saw the light in his eyes. She'd broken through that crusty exterior and this was the man beneath it. She liked it. Maybe this wouldn't go so badly after all.

Slowly she made it up the walk and to the front steps with John's help. The front door opened and a very curious Jacob was standing there.

"Hello, Miss O'Bryne."

"Hello, Jacob."

He exchanged glances with his father and then gave her another look of consideration. "Did you hurt yourself?"

"Even those of us who have trained our entire lives don't always focus enough and this is what happens."

He nodded as she passed by and into the house.

"I thought I'd thrill her with macaroni and cheese for dinner. That should make her feel better right?" John asked as he mussed Jacob's hair with his hand.

"Can I get you anything, Miss O'Bryne?"

Kym turned and smiled at him. "First of all, let's make a deal. When I'm in your house you can call me Kym. Is that okay?"

"Yes, ma'am," he answered hesitantly.

John moved to her side. "Your choice, you can sit in the living room and watch Disney Channel or come in the kitchen were I'm going to boil water and noodles."

"I'll come with you."

They'd taken a few more steps when a woman emerged from the other room with Cody on her hip.

"Oh, John! Who do you have with you?"

"Mom, this is Kym O'Bryne."

His mother's eyes grew wide. "Oh! You are as cute as your grandfather said you were."

"Thank you, Mrs. Larson."

"Oh, it's Evie." She looked at her standing next to the enormous John. "Are you hurt?"

"Just twisted my knee this afternoon. It'll be fine in a few days."

"Don't count on it. But my John's late wife taught him everything there is to know about wrapping up injuries, and Lord knows he's had his share."

John let out an audible breath. "Okay, Mom. She doesn't need to know I'm a hazard."

Kym tucked her lips between her teeth to keep the smile and laughter at bay.

"I suppose I should get home and get your father's dinner started." She handed Cody to John. "He's already had a bath because he got into that mud pit by the back door."

He kissed Cody's head. "You're a trouble maker for Grandma, aren't you?"

Cody simply rested his head on his father's shoulder.

Evie stepped in to kiss John on the cheek and then she looked at Kym. "It was nice to meet you. I hope to see you around."

"It was nice to meet you as well."

Evie gave a little hum of satisfaction and walked out of the room.

"Are you okay with rumor mills?" John whispered.

"Why?"

"You just met one," he said as he started toward the other room which she assumed was the kitchen.

Kym wasn't very thrilled with his last statement. Seriously, was she to believe his own mother would start rumors about them?

Jacob was walking slowly through the house behind her. "Is everything alright, Jacob?"

"Yes. I'm just here if you need my help."

"You've very sweet. I'm just a little slow, but I'll be okay."

John had set Cody down and pulled a kitchen chair around so that she could sit and prop up her leg. She didn't like being waited on and she knew that Jacob was very uncomfortable having her around, but this was what it was to date a man with a family. She'd been in awkward situations before and she'd survived. She'd survive this one too. And, maybe, just maybe, it would pay off at the end of the night with one of those toe curling, amazing kisses that John could give. Even the thought of it made her stomach warm.

Kym sat down in the chair he offered and he moved the other chair close so she could rest her leg on it.

"Jacob, go get a pillow for her to rest her knee on."

He nodded and left the room.

"You don't have to go through all of this for me."

John rested his hand on her arm. "I want to."

Jacob returned and handed her the pillow. "Thank you."

He nodded nervously.

"How much homework do you have tonight?" John asked as he took a pot out from under the stove and set it in the sink to fill.

"Spelling and math."

"Why don't you get started on that?"

There was the unmistakable groan of disappointment.

Kym reached out and touched his arm. "What kind of math?"

"Division and word problems."

She scrunched up her face. "I'm up for a challenge. Can I try it with you?"

Jacob wrinkled his nose. "You want to do math for fun?"

"Sure."

"Okay, if you want to." He headed toward the coat rack by the back door and took down his backpack. He pulled out the papers and walked back to the table. "I'll get some extra paper." He left the room and Kym smiled up at John.

"I'm about to embarrass myself."

John shook his head. "I doubt that. Something tells me you're pretty smart."

"You're about to find out that math is not my strong point."

"You have many others," he said softly right before Jacob walked back in.

As John fixed three boxes of macaroni and cheese Jacob proved that he was much better in math than Kym was. Every time she took a moment too long or even got the wrong answer Jacob did a small celebration dance.

"I told you I wasn't very good at math."

"You're right," Jacob said enthusiastically and then his face turned hard. "I'm sorry. That wasn't nice."

"I'll let it slide. Your homework is done and you had a good time doing it. I'll be gracious enough to accept defeat."

He smiled.

John placed a pot holder in the center of the kitchen table and then returned again with a huge pot of macaroni and cheese. "Go get your brothers and your sister. Wash your hands."

"Yes, sir."

Jacob gathered his homework and tucked it back into his backpack.

Kym lowered her leg and tried to stand. She was wobbly, but John had hurried over to her.

"What are you doing?"

"Washing my hands before dinner. But my leg seems to have stiffened."

John reached down and touched her knee. "It's really swollen. You can't train on that tomorrow."

"It won't be the first time I've taught class from the sidelines."

He helped her to the sink. "You've done this a lot?"

"This is just a small sprain. I'll get over this. When I dislocated it, that was a bit more recovery."

"And what were you doing when you dislocated it?" he asked resting his hand in the small of her back as she turned on the sink to wash her hands.

"Run, jump, side kick through three boards."

"You did four yesterday."

"So I did," her voice was airy with his breath in her ear.

"Daddy, I weady," Cody toddled into the kitchen.

John's hand left her body instantly and he picked up his son and set him in the high chair which he then pushed up to the table. "Where are the others?"

"Bafwoom."

Kym laughed at his little words.

"C'mon. Let's eat," John shouted and helped her back to the table.

Dinner was every bit as chaotic as John had promised her. But Kym hadn't run or even looked frightened. Maybe she was a keeper.

Jacob, on the other hand, was on the quiet side.

When they were finished the family spread out through the house.

"They don't have after dinner chores?"

"They are very little and Jacob does quite a bit around here. I let him off the hook after dinner."

She nodded slowly. "You don't think that gives them the wrong idea?"

John ran water in the sink and added soap. "Meaning?"

"I'm just saying that even Cody can take a rag to something. It gives them some worth to help out."

He ran his tongue over his teeth. People had been telling him how to raise his kids for years and now she was too. "I suppose you think I should reward them with money too? Allowance?"

"Heavens no. They live in this house too. There are some things you just do." As she sat with her knee up, and now a frozen bag of peas draped over it at his urging, she was scraping bowls into a single bowl so there was less for him to do. "I'm just saying kids complain, but they want to be part of the bigger picture."

"Do you know what would happen right now if I told Mason to come in here and do what you're doing?"

"He'd throw a fit."

He hadn't really expected her to give him the right answer. As far as he was concerned she was just talking about things she didn't know about.

"Well, yeah. I'm tired. I'm not in the mood for a fit."

"Okay. So he throws a fit for a week. And then next week before he ever leaves the table he's collected a few bowls and dishes and walked them over to you. He's gained a sense of worth for what he has. And *if* you tell him thank you, he'll have a sense that he's done right by you."

John rubbed his chin with his hand only to realize he needed a shave and his hand was still wet. He took the towel, dried off his face and then set it on the counter.

"If you're so wise how do you suppose I should begin this *chore* thing?"

She was smiling and he hated it. Oh, she had the most beautiful smile and it lit up her green eyes. But she was about to make an ass of him and he didn't know if he was ready for that or not.

"Give me three more chores that you do every night?"

"Trash. Sweep the floor. Dry dishes."

She nodded. "I'll guarantee one of those chores you'll have to do when they are all done. But I promise you, even Cody will try."

"Okay hot shot." John walked to the doorway and looked at all four of his kids contently watching some show about wizards. Cody watched as he sat on an old plastic rocking horse that he was out growing. Mason lay on the ground on his tummy and kicked the couch with his feet. Abby had a doll in her lap she was absent mindedly combing her hair. And Jacob, well, by the look of him, he'd been paying much too much attention to the conversation John had been having with Kym. He was on to them already, John could tell.

"You guys come in here for a minute," he announced and all four of them turned to just look at him. "I'm serious. Come in here. Kym has some new things to share with you."

He turned to see her narrow her gaze at him.

Slowly all four of them walked into the room. Cody clung right to John's leg. Oh, this wasn't going to be pretty. It wasn't really fair to make his kids not like her, but she'd won them over before—even without his help—she'd win them over again, he was sure of it.

Kim took the peas off her knee and set her foot gently on the ground. From where she sat in the chair she was eye level with almost all of them.

"I was talking to your dad and I told him that you guys should be in here helping him after dinner each night. If he had some help he could spend a few more minutes a night with you." She was nodding as she spoke softly. "So from now on everyone is going to help with dinner clean up. This will be your job until your dad decides to change them. Yes, ma'am?"

Jacob answered first with Abby following right behind. "Yes, ma'am."

He was going to have to try that giving the required command with the directions. He'd seen it work more than once this week on his own kids.

"Jacob, since you're strong, your job will be to take out the trash each night and put a new bag in the trash can, yes ma'am?"

"Yes, ma'am."

She gave him a nod and looked at Abby. "Miss Abby, your job is to help your father do the dishes. You dry them for him after he washes them, yes, ma'am?"

"Yes, ma'am."

Again Kym smiled at her before looking at Mason. "Mason, you look strong too."

He nodded to agree.

"Do you see what I did with all the bowls we used at dinner tonight? I scraped all the food out of them into one bowl. And the few bits of milk left in cups, I poured them into one cup. Do you think you can do that?"

Mason looked at her and then his father. John nodded and Mason in returned nodded toward Kym.

"Remember in class we talked about how we answer our elders?"

He crinkled up his nose and thought for a moment. "Yes, Miss ma'am."

"Close enough." She rested a gentle hand on his shoulder.

Cody had let go of his father's leg and moved toward her. This was mutiny, John thought. That voodoo she had she was using it again.

"Cody, can you sweep the floor?"

Cody nodded and grinned.

"You can do that for your daddy every night?"

He nodded again.

"Can you say yes ma'am?"

"Yep!"

Kym laughed. "Well that'll work for tonight." She looked up at John with a smug smile of satisfaction on those rosy lips. "And if you get me a rag I'll wipe down the table and the counters. I did eat here too."

In less than ten minutes the chores in the kitchen were done and Kym was wiping down the table. As each child had finished their appointed job she'd thanked them, which had prompted the reminder that he do the same. No one had argued and he was sure one of them would.

"What do you want for dinner tomorrow?" He asked as he put away the last of the mostly dried dishes.

"You're afraid they won't volunteer tomorrow to do this."

"I can guarantee it."

She laughed easily around him now and he liked that. He'd been afraid she'd be edgy and afraid that he'd bounce between pleasant and horrible as he always did. But she made him want to be happy. Abigail had made him that way too.

He caught himself when he began to compare the two. There was nothing alike about them, except that they were good, caring women.

Well, that wasn't a bad quality to share between the women he loved.

He turned back to put away another dish. He couldn't have her looking at him, knowing he'd even thought about that emotion.

Kym O'Bryne was still a stranger. Love was for people who put in years of time and commitment to a relationship. Maybe in time he'd consider love. For now he just wanted to consider that she was willing to spend time with him—and his kids.

She limped across the kitchen with the rag in her hand and gracefully she draped it over the divider in the sink. "Thank you for a wonderful dinner, Mr. Larson. I had a wonderful evening."

"Unique dining experience?"

"In the most pleasant of ways," she said softly stepping closer to him.

He wanted to gather her up in his arms and see how wonderful a kiss could be when both of them moved in for it together. But it was too risky right now. Those amazingly wonderful kids of his were just around the corner and that eight-year-old was already suspicious.

She must have had the same thought because she took a step back and rested against the counter.

"I'd like to present the kids with uniforms tomorrow. Would you be okay with that?"

"As long as you're still not charging me and they still want to go, you can give them whatever you want to."

"They've earned them. I'm very proud of how hard they've been working."

He leaned against the counter too, facing her. "This isn't just a way to support child labor is it? I don't want to have to turn you in."

She smiled again. "Your kitchen will be your own chore again if you do."

"Point taken. I'll try to be there to see them get their uniforms."

She was batting her eyes now. He'd made her tear up. How did he do that?

"I should head home. You have more evening routines to continue."

He wanted to ask her to stay. Share bath time and bed time with them. Even if she didn't stay all night, to have her there…was for another time, he quickly realized.

"I'll walk you out."

Kym had said goodbye to the kids and even Cody had hugged onto her good leg and didn't want to let go. But it worried her when Jacob said goodnight to her. He had a shift in his reaction to her—as mistrust had formed. Hopefully she could make it go away.

John had put on his coat and shut the front door behind him.

"You'd better get back in there. If you're out here too long they're going to be looking out windows."

"I'm sure the neighbors are already doing that."

She'd lived in big cities and small towns, but neighbors in all of them were alike—they wanted to know what was going on.

"Thank you for today. I've had quite an adventure."

He reached for her hand and interlaced their fingers. "It's been a busy day."

"Maybe tomorrow will be a bit more quiet."

He nodded. "I don't care what kind of day it is as long as I see you."

"That's right. You did say if you kissed me it meant I was yours."

He pursed his lips. "Not as a possession. It just means writing you a note that asks if you'll be my girlfriend check yes or no is a little immature."

"Oh, I don't know. That's cute."

His eyes met hers in the dark and a million words passed between them without either of them uttering a one.

Commitment. Relationship. Family. Business. Kids. Love…were just a few. They both knew there were a million components that would need to fall in place for this to work out. They were one day into an uncertain relationship, but Kym wanted this. Oh, last week she'd all but hated the man, but right now she couldn't find the strength to even leave his sight.

"Goodnight, John." She opened the door to her car.

"Goodnight, Kym," he said softly bending down to kiss her cheek ever so gently.

It was going to have to do, she knew that. She climbed in her car and started it.

The curtain in the living room shifted as she drove away. He'd known what he was doing. They were being watched. She needed to remember those four people came before her. She should be used to it. She was the only daughter among strong and handsome sons. Every day of her life she had to prove that she was a strong and smart woman. This would be no different.

As John's house faded from view she already missed him—missed them.

Patience. She had enormous amounts of patience. But committing to John Larson was going to take all the patience she had—she wanted it all right now.

Chapter Eleven

Pain shot through Kym's knee as she tried to walk. This was not good. It had swollen during the night.

She managed her way to the kitchen where her grandfather sat, a cup of tea in his hands, a cup near her empty chair.

"You are injured."

"I twisted my knee last night when I was training."

He gave her a slow nod. "Your mind is not in focus."

Kym managed her way to her chair and sat down. "I'm going to need to call in some help today. I'm going to have a hard time teaching."

Her grandfather nodded slowly. "I will teach."

She knew not to doubt him. To doubt her grandfather would only prove to be a mistake that would cost her dearly.

"I'd appreciate that."

He lifted his chin. "Tell me about the man."

Now, not only her knee hurt, but her heart ached too. This was not a conversation she wanted to have with her grandfather, but she couldn't walk away now. He already knew.

"I assume you mean Mr. Larson." He gave her a bow of his head and then turned his ear toward her so he could hear.

"He was kind enough to change the filter in the furnace and get the windows open in the back of the school. Then he invited me over for dinner at his house. With his children," she was sure to add.

"Ah, he has many children."

"Four."

"His wife died."

Proof that her grandfather had melded into this little town better than she had.

"Yes."

"A man with so many children will find it hard to put a woman first."

Kym gritted her teeth. "Yes. I know that."

"But a woman who could take on a man and his young children would have to be very kind of heart and very full of patience."

She let her shoulders drop. "Yes."

He patted her hand and stood from his chair. "You, my Kym, have both."

He left her sitting alone at the table, his compliment still buzzing in her head. Kind of heart and full of patience. The thought brought a smile to her face. The patience wasn't needed with the younger children. They would either like her or they wouldn't. But Jacob would need her patience.

Kym had been teaching long enough to see families come together and others fall apart. She knew that he liked her, but did her like her enough to let her be part of his father's life? And she needed to be very honest with herself. Did *she* want to be part of his father's life?

She'd seen his less than cheery disposition on more than one occasion. But she'd seen his compassion too. And when he kissed her, she'd felt the depth of his passion.

Kym rested her head in her hands. That morning he'd run into her at the grocery store, she never could have imagined she'd be losing sleep over him or wanting to see him every moment. But she had and she did.

Love was not a foreign feeling to her. She'd been in love. They'd even spoken of marriage, but things were not meant for them. And why not? They were both single, business minded people. He'd had no baggage where as

John Larson had plenty. Why didn't love work for her before? And how would it work with four kids and the memory of a late wife?

The throbbing in her knee drew her back into the moment. She needed to get some ice on it and wrap it.

As she hobbled from her chair to the refrigerator she heard what sounded like tiny rocks against the patio door. Carefully she maneuvered to the door and looked out. Below her stood John crouched down picking up another handful of tiny pebbles from the ground.

She opened the door. "What are you doing?" She laughed as she inched out onto the patio in her robe.

"I don't have your phone number."

"This is a bit old fashioned isn't it?"

"You don't have a trellis."

She laughed and cinched up her robe against the cold. "Why don't you come up?"

John looked around and then shook his head. "You'd better come down." He tucked his hands into his pockets. "I was going to go visit Wil at the hospital before they're released. Thought you might like to go."

First he'd kissed her, then he'd taken her home to be with his children, now he was offering a public outing. The cold air stuck in her lungs. This was what she'd wanted. But it was happening too fast—but that was what she'd wanted too.

Then the reality of it hit—they were only going to visit friends. It wasn't as if they were going on a date.

"I have to change."

John nodded. "I'll wait."

She turned to go back inside, limping as she moved toward the door.

"You're still limping," he called up.

"It's really swollen."

"Good thing we're going to the hospital."

It had taken Kym nearly twenty minutes to come downstairs after he'd thrown rocks at her window. By the look on her face she was only mildly surprised to find him standing there in the front of the school holding a mug of hot tea.

"My grandfather?"

John nodded. "I think he took pity on me standing out here in the cold."

She touched his arm. "It means a great deal more than that."

He assumed it did, but he wasn't going to be the one making those kinds of accusations.

She took the mug from him and set it on the front counter. "I'll take this up later. Do we have enough time to go to the florist? I don't want to visit empty handed."

The florist? Couldn't she have wanted to take something else? No.

"Yeah, sure."

She was studying him and then she smiled. "Oh, John Larson, there is a story with you and the florist."

"You're not so wise."

She grinned again as they walked out of the school and she turned and locked the door.

Her knee was obviously hurting her, especially in the cold. It was a great excuse to scoop her up, throw her over his shoulder, and carry her to the car—which was what he did.

Kym squealed in laughter. "I can walk."

"This is more fun."

"Don't you slip on the ice or I'll have a concussion too."

When he reached the truck he set her down. "I guess if you get a concussion you can't work."

She narrowed her eyes on him. "I suppose you'd be right. That would cause for a world of hurt in my life."

Right. They were both independently employed. Taking time off wasn't even a consideration. And why had he even said it? He hadn't left Aspen Creek for more than a few days at a time at any given time. When his father owned the hardware store they couldn't go on vacation then either. But every minute he spent with this woman he wanted another. And every moment he spent away from her he ached for the minute he'd see her again. This hadn't happened to him in a long time.

He opened the door for her and she managed to climb in. When she was settled he shut the door, walked to the other side, and climbed in.

The truck had been off long enough that the heat in the cab had gone. "It'll take her a second to get warm again."

"I'll be fine."

"The grocery store has some nice bouquets," he said as he backed out of the parking lot.

That sexy grin was back on her lips and it was hard to focus on the icy road ahead of him.

"I haven't gotten around town too much. So what is her name?"

"Whose?"

"The woman at the florist."

John ran his tongue over his teeth. "Heather."

"And I assume you dated her before you met your wife?"

"Who said I dated her?" He turned down Main Street and the back of the truck fishtailed slightly on the frozen ground.

"You didn't date her?"

"No."

He pulled up in front of the store. Heather had already set out the decorations for the holidays. She always was the first to do so. Though she said it was because it brought in business, he was sure there were other reasons.

Kym smiled as he put the truck in park. "I'll be just a moment."

He only gave her a nod. She was a quick study on people. No matter how crass or crabby he was, she was kind hearted enough to understand that going inside wasn't something he wanted to do.

Kym carefully hopped out of the truck and limped into the store.

Through the window he could see the exchange. Heather smiled and welcomed Kym and Kym seemed to have worked that magic where she had put Heather at ease. When he saw both of them turn and look at him he knew that he'd become part of the conversation.

There was a stabbing sensation in his gut. Guilt—it was guilt. There was no reason he should be cowering in his truck.

With a groan he turned off the engine and stepped out of the truck.

The women stopped chatting when he opened the door and the little bell he'd hung there rang.

Heather's smile left her eyes. "Good morning, John."

"Heather."

She turned back to Kym. "Give Wil my best. She'll enjoy these. They're her favorite kind of flower."

"I'm sure she will. And thank you so much. Your shop is beautiful."

"Thank you."

John took the vase from Kym and lent her his arm to steady herself. He opened the door and as she passed through it he turned and looked back at Heather.

"The drain pipe on the side of the building came apart again. I'll stop by and fix it for you. Make sure nothing leaked behind the cooler," he said as he shut the door behind him.

They climbed into his truck. Kym balanced the vase on her lap. John started the truck, with some hesitation from the engine, and backed out of the lot.

She was being quiet. Too quiet. What did Heather tell her? She wasn't in there long enough for her to have completely turned Kym against him. But would she really do that to him? Yes, she just might.

The hospital was only another three minutes away. If there was any salvation in living in a small town it was that that awkward silence between two people in a car didn't have to last for long.

John pulled up to the hospital and parked. The hum of the engine died when he turned off the truck. Now it was too silent.

"I'll help you out," he said and she reached for him.

"Tell me who she is."

John gnawed on his lip. There was nothing to hide. He wasn't embarrassed or ashamed. It just hurt.

"Heather?" He asked and Kym nodded. "Abigail's sister."

Kym's eyes softened. "I assumed she was a relative. Pictures of the kids are hanging by the register."

"I didn't know she had those." He decided he'd take a new set of school pictures with him when he went back to fix the drain pipe.

"Why the hesitation?" She asked as she pulled her hand back and touched one of the gentle petals of the tulips Heather had arranged for Wil.

John rubbed the back of his neck which was hot with sweat even sitting in the cab of the old truck which was growing very cold.

"Abigail wanted three kids." He rubbed at his eyes which had begun to sting. "I wanted four."

Kym was silent. This was that voodoo wasn't it? He'd be spilling his guts in 5-4-3-2...

"I begged her for another baby until she gave in and it killed her."

Kym reached for him again. His reaction was to pull away, but he fought that too.

"Heather and her mother blame me for her death. She'd still be here if I hadn't needed that last child. If I'd just been happy with life the way it was Abigail would be here."

"Do you feel that way?" she asked and her voice was soft.

He sucked in a breath of cold air. "Yes."

Kym's face tensed, though he was sure she wasn't aware of it. "Cody wasn't a mistake."

"I know."

"He's a joyous little boy who needs his family."

"I know that," he snapped.

Her hand still rested on his arm and she gave him a squeeze. "Then make peace with it."

"Peace with what? That I caused her to die because I wanted him?"

"Unless you did something to cause her to die then it was the way it was supposed to be."

He turned forcing her to remove her hand. "The way it was supposed to be? One life for another? I loved my wife.

The reason to have more kids was to have a full house. Full of the love we had. Not to have this existence where my kids lost her."

"I just think you're wrong to blame yourself."

"Didn't you hear me? I'm not the only one who blames me. The kids have an aunt and a grandmother who don't like me either. How is that harmony?"

"John…"

"Well now you know. I *am* an S-O-B and that's the way of it." He opened the door and it creaked in protest.

Kym sat still, paralyzed in her seat. She had only wanted to get Wil flowers, but now she's caused a whole scene. But how was she to know?

John pulled open her door and reached for the vase. "C'mon. They'll be home with the baby before we get in there."

He held out his hand to help her down and she climbed out of the truck.

John held on to her as she limped through the snow in the parking lot and though the doors of the hospital. Then he let her walk on her own.

Her knee throbbed and her heart hurt. There was no possible way that this little relationship they were forming was going to work out when he could easily get so upset over his wife. And she didn't blame him, but she wanted to.

Wil was asleep when they got to the room, but a very quiet Christopher sat in the corner rocking their baby.

"Come in," he whispered.

Kym limped in with John just a few steps behind her. She set the vase on the dresser. "These are for Malory."

"She loves tulips."

"Heather mentioned it," she said and then noticed the men exchanged uneasy glances at each other. The moment only made her feel smaller. She should have just gone to the grocery store.

"Oh, hey," a groggy Malory said as she forced her eyes open and sat up in bed.

Malory looked tired, and who would blame her?

"Congratulations," Kym whispered as if that were the only way to communicate around a sleeping infant. "I brought you some tulips."

"My favorite." She smiled, her head still rested against the pillow.

"You look good, Wil," John said in a full voice, but the baby didn't stir. Kym realized he'd have known she wouldn't.

"Thanks, John." She smiled at him.

Kym felt very out of place with the situation. These people had been friends since childhood. She assumed they were there to help John through his darkest times when he lost Abigail. She was an intruder into their circle.

"Kym, would you like to hold her?" Christopher said standing with the baby in his arms.

"Oh, I don't…"

"Of course she does," John answered for her. "You should have seen her with Cade and Olivia's little guy."

Christopher laughed. "That one will be a linebacker I'll betcha."

While they bantered about the baby of other childhood friends, John was guiding her to the chair. She sat down and Christopher handed her his daughter.

"She's beautiful."

"Yeah. Looks just like her mother," Chris said softly.

That tugged at Kym's heart. John sat on the arm of the chair and leaned over them.

"You're getting better at holding these little guys."

She looked up at him and the anger which had clouded his eyes was now gone. He was used to dealing with the pain of losing his wife. But it didn't ease Kym's hurt feelings.

"Kym, why were you limping?" Malory asked.

She looked up. "I sprained my knee yesterday."

"That reminds me," John said as he stood up from the chair and walked out of the room.

He was a mystery. Who was this man and why did she care so much about him?

Christopher sat on the edge of Malory's bed and made small talk with Kym until John returned with a man following close behind wearing a doctor's coat over blue scrubs.

"Kym, this is Greg Meyers. He's going to look at your knee."

"Oh, thank you, but..."

"He owes me." John smiled.

"Yeah, he fixed the roof last week saving me thousands in damage. He's just that kind of guy."

Kym looked up at John who didn't like the compliments she was finding. But he was this gracious man rolled into a hard, crusty exterior. And she was falling in love with him harder as he tried to shrug away the compliments.

"Here, I'll take her," John said taking the baby from her arms.

Greg went about lifting Kym's pant leg and looking at her knee. He then came back and wrapped it so that it was tight and protected. He gave her instruction on taking care of it and within fifteen minutes he was on his way to treat someone else and he'd done it all as a favor for the man who unselfishly fixed his roof—for free—because his family needed it.

This little town embraced this broken man. But was she the woman who could even fill that void? She was an outsider in a circle where everyone grew up together and knew everything about the other. No one knew Kym O'Bryne. Sometimes she wondered if she even knew herself.

Chapter Twelve

There was an ease in her step now that Greg had fixed Kym up. John was glad it had been Greg who had been on duty when he'd walked out to find one of the two doctors on call. The other doctor, who was as old as the town John figured, wasn't as easy to convince about giving favors.

John opened the door for her and Kym climbed into the truck.

"Does your knee feel better?"

"Much. Thank you."

"He used to play doctor with Kelley when we were little. And I don't mean it in the terms adults use. I mean he had her bandaged up all the time." He laughed at the memory. "I knew he'd take care of you."

Kym reached for him and touched his cheek. "You had taken good care of me."

John swallowed hard. He backed away and shut the door.

He thought about the past few days as he steadied himself against his truck to keep from falling on the ice. The day he'd run into Kym O'Bryne in the grocery store he hadn't expected to have his life change. In fact, he'd hoped to have never had to have crossed paths with her again— but here he was.

The door creaked as he pulled it open and climbed inside the truck, which was bitter cold.

Kym was looking at her phone and sending a text as he started up the engine. He looked at her before he began backing out of the lot.

"You look perplexed. Is everything okay?" he asked.

She turned her head and plastered on an obviously forced smile. "Yes. I just got a text from my brother. He's flying in on Monday to collect my grandfather for Thanksgiving. It looks as though he'll be flying to Ireland with him."

Her voice had shaken as he told her about the plans her family had made.

"You weren't expecting that?"

"No." She tucked her phone back into her coat pocket. "My grandfather is ninety years old. That's quite a journey for a man his age."

"Yes," John said as he turned down Main Street. "But he doesn't seem ailing at all."

She nodded. "I know. It's just…" She bit down on her lip and then looked out the window. "I hadn't thought much about Thanksgiving, but without my grandfather here it means I'll be alone." She quickly turned to him and held up a hand. "And I don't mind that."

Her gesture stung. Perhaps she anticipated him inviting her over and she didn't want to. That was fine. Just because the woman was occupying his every thought didn't mean he had to drag her further into his life. Thanksgiving dinner was a big commitment.

"It'll be nice to see my brother," she continued. "But you do understand what this really means don't you?"

John shook his head as he drove back toward her school.

"It means that when my grandfather leaves here and goes back to Ireland with my mother I'll probably never see him again."

He noticed the first tear roll down her cheek and she turned from him and quickly wiped it away.

What did John know about being alone? Even when his wife died he was anything but alone. He had four children to take care of. His mother had been at his house every day and his mother-in-law stuck her nose in there too. His father took over at the store until he'd had another heart attack and his sister did everything she could to make sure he had some ounce of sanity left. Chris took him hunting, upon protest, but it had been good to get away. But he'd never been alone.

Then it hit him. Maybe she didn't want to stay in his little town. What if she wanted to go with her grandfather? The entire conversation replayed in his head.

John's hands twitched on the steering wheel. He pursed his lips and planned out his next sentence so that it wouldn't sound as if he were worried. "Do you want to go back to Ireland?"

"No."

Her answer was quick and solid. That gave him a bit of peace.

"How about where your brothers live?"

Kym shifted toward him as he pulled up in front of her school. "If I didn't know better I would think you wanted me to leave Aspen Creek."

"No." His answer was equally as quick and solid. "I just feel bad that you'll be all alone."

"Well, I'm ready to start my life without my family hovering. I've always had someone looking out for me as if I couldn't do things on my own. I was surprised when they bought this school and wanted me to run it. But I wasn't really surprised that Grandfather came with the deal." The sadness in her eyes had lifted and now there was a fire. "I was the only daughter. I have fought harder than those two numb-skull brothers of mine. Trust me, in this industry a woman can be faster, stronger, and better than any man— but she's still at the bottom of the pile."

She'd intertwined her fingers in her lap.

"Always, either my father was there to *supervise* me or one of my brothers was. This is my chance to make this school whatever I want it to be. And right now I think it's doing just that. It's providing a service to the community. And I have ideas—lots of ideas on how to incorporate the town into more than just martial arts. There is so much more."

Her voice had lifted in an anger infused excitement that made him smile. Oh, he could pick them. The strong opinionated ones. Kym was no different.

"So you'll be staying in Aspen Creek?"

She let out a grand sigh and laughed. "Yes."

"Good. Because I think Jacob has a long way to go with his training."

"Is that so?"

"Mason told him about all the boards you broke. I don't think there is a piece of furniture in my house that is safe now."

"I guess I'd better let him try then." She looked out the window at the school. "I suppose I'd better get ready for classes this afternoon."

"Yeah. I'd better go fix that drain at the flower shop."

"You still take care of Abigail's sister, even though she's not nice to you?"

"It's not her fault. Abigail was all she had. She deserves to feel ripped off."

"Is that how you feel? Ripped off?"

"Damn straight." It didn't feel right telling her that, but she didn't seem upset by the thought.

"You're grumpy on the outside, but you're a softy on the inside."

"Don't tell anyone. I have a rep to uphold."

She smiled again. "Your secret is safe with me John Larson."

He nodded and then opened his door, jumped out, and walked around to let her out of the truck.

She took his hand and gently slid out and carefully balanced on her stable foot before setting the other on the ground. "It really does feel better," she said balancing her weight on both feet.

"Good. Don't go hurting yourself."

"I won't."

John stood there looking down at her. This was the part about falling for someone that he didn't do well with—the separation. He had work to do and he'd goofed around all morning. But seeing her nose grow pink in the cold, he didn't want to leave her. He just wanted to wrap her up in his arms, warm her, and kiss her for the rest of the day.

But that wasn't going to do.

"When is your last class?"

Kym hunched up her shoulders as if to have them shield the cold from her neck and ears. "At eight. I close up the school after nine."

That would complicate things a bit. "I'll come and pick up Jacob and Abby."

"If you ever need them to stay…"

"Thanks." Wasn't that like everyone else? Always thinking that was the most helpful way? "I'll be here."

"Thank you for taking me to see Wil."

John took a step back and scanned a look over her with a smile. "Oh, hell, you're really stuck here now aren't you?"

"Why?"

"You just called her Wil."

Kym laughed. "So I did." She stepped up closer to him. "I guess this town and its citizens are growing on me."

John forced down the knot in his throat. "I'll see you later." He kissed her on the cheek.

There was a bit of disappointment in her eyes, but she smiled as she walked past him and into the building.

He was going to need to have a long talk with his kids. The aching in his chest wasn't from the cold. It was from the warmth that surged through him every time he thought about spending time with Kym. That was a warmth he never thought he'd feel again after Abigail died.

How was a man truly supposed to move on from that?

How did Abigail feel?

John dropped his shoulders, shut the door on the truck, and walked to the other side.

Certainly he was losing his mind if he wondered how his dead wife felt. He climbed into the truck and backed out of the lot.

The leak at the flower shop, that's what he needed to focus on.

Maybe when he was done he'd take some flowers to Abigail. On more than one occasion over the past few years she'd helped him with some decisions. He guessed that if she didn't like his seeing Kym she'd somehow let him know.

But that thought scared the hell out of him. What if she really didn't want him to see her? He wasn't sure he could deal with that.

Chapter Thirteen

That stupid bell over the door rang again announcing his presence. John closed the door behind him as Heather walked out of the back room, an enormous smile plastered on her face ready to greet her customer. But the moment she saw him her eyes turned hard and the smile was only a memory.

"Didn't think you meant today," she growled.

"It shouldn't wait." He walked over toward the cooler. "Nothing leaked behind here did it?" He couldn't see any damage, but he thought it was safer to keep her talking than for her to come up behind him and stab him in the back.

"It's dry."

He nodded. "Okay. I'll get it fixed up." He walked back to the door and with his hand on the knob and his back turned to her he said, "Can you make me up a little bouquet, you know…her favorite."

He didn't say anything more and he didn't wait for an answer.

The wind had picked up in the valley making the chill in the air burn his skin and freeze him through to the inside. Fixing the drain wouldn't take too long and he could see Heather inside making up the bouquet he'd requested.

He despised this anger that wouldn't settle between them. It had almost been three years and still the woman would rather hate him than be his comfort.

Before Abigail died, he and Heather were good friends. He'd chased off the bad guys and he'd set her up with a few good ones. They had each other's back. And the moment Abigail took her last breath he'd been banished from her family.

Of course she'd remained civil enough around the kids, but usually when he walked into the store the curses flew and her voice teetered on the brink of breaking the sound barrier it was so loud and high.

But he'd continue to suffer her wrath for his children. They loved her and their grandmother. By the time Cody was eighteen, John wouldn't have to worry about it anymore. The kids would be on their own to socialize with Abigail's family, but that wasn't really how he wanted it.

John had been right about the job, it hadn't taken long. He was a big believer in fixing it early so there wouldn't be bigger problems. The building was old and he'd nearly replaced every part of it over the years. He was proud of the little shop. They'd worked hard to make it what it was and Heather took great care of it.

When he'd tucked his tools away in his truck he headed back into the store.

Heather leaned against the counter, her arms crossed over her chest. The anger had diffused from her eyes, which he'd known would happen too. He'd come to learn that the spark of anger was when she saw him and that raw nerve of missing her sister hit her. Eventually the acknowledgement that he'd lost someone very important too broke through. It usually didn't make her any nicer to him, but perhaps a little quieter.

"I added a candy cane lily. You know how she liked the holidays," she added as if maybe he'd forgotten.

"She'll enjoy that."

"The kids are going to be able to come over for Thanksgiving dinner, right?" She was biting down on her lip.

"Of course."

"What about you?"

That one threw him for a bit of a loop. "Me? We're eating early at Mom's. I'll have had my dinner."

She shifted her eyes away from him. "So what's with you and that woman you brought in?"

There it was. This had nothing to do with Thanksgiving at all. She was teetering on that fence of irritation with him over Kym. This was more comfortable.

"We were headed to see Wil. She wanted flowers."

"And you thought it was a good idea to bring her here?"

"Nope." He shook his head. "I told her they had nice arrangements at the store too."

"Those are my arrangements."

"She still would have gotten quality."

Heather narrowed her eyes. "You're seeing her?"

"I'm trying."

"Trying? What does that really mean?" Her voice was rising. "Either you are or you aren't, John."

"Then I guess I am."

She slammed her hands to the counter. "And what about my sister?"

John usually would turn and walk away, but he knew Heather and somehow she'd take it to Kym. That wasn't going to happen.

"Well, if you must know I was headed up to have a conversation with your sister about this."

"Funny. Real funny."

"I'm not laughing." He said with his eyes focused on her.

Her wall of anger visibly diffused. "It's too soon."

"It's almost been three years."

"She loved you."

"And I still love her." He moved closer to the counter. "I'm not trying to move on and forget her. I'm not even trying to replace her in my kids' lives. But Kym happened into my life and I like her. I really like her. When I'm with her some of the pain goes away. But it will always be there."

Heather was battling her emotions behind her eyes which were now filling with tears. "Don't forget my sister."

"How can I? I have four children with her eyes. One with her name." He reached his hand out and covered hers. "There will never be another Abigail."

"I can hardly turn around during this time of year without thinking about her."

Now John smiled. "The shop looks great."

"She loved Christmas."

"She sure did. You do a great job keeping that part of her alive."

Heather sucked in a breath and her eyes dried quickly. She pulled her hand away from John's and took a step back. "Go have your talk then. Maybe you'll fall off the side of the mountain if she doesn't like your idea."

And she was back. John gave her a nod. "Better make sure you stay in town for the next hour. If someone sees you up there they'll think you pushed me."

She let out a snort.

"How much do I owe you for the flowers?" he asked.

"You own the damn store. You don't have to pay for them."

"I have to cover the cost of the product."

She shook her head and walked away from the counter and back to the room where she created the masterpieces.

John took a twenty out of his pocket and threw it on the counter.

He turned and left the small store his wife had wanted so badly and had spent so many hours of her short life building it to be perfect.

The frozen layer of snow crunched under John's boots as he walked toward Abigail's grave high above Aspen Creek. The cemetery dated back to Aspen Creek's beginning. There were mothers and fathers of John's friends. His own grandparents, on both sides. There were the rich and famous. There were John and Jane Does. Among them was Abigail Larson.

John knelt down in the snow and brushed off her headstone. He'd known it was hers by the flowers that still jaunted up from the ground which were now frozen and muted in color.

He removed the old flowers and set new ones in the vase. In the cold, without water, they surely would freeze in a day as well. But it helped his heart to visit her and bring them.

A chilly breeze blew through the cemetery and he knew she was there with him, in her own way. He laughed as he stood against the wind. It hadn't knocked him over the cliff.

"Heather decorated the store just like you liked it. Thanksgiving isn't even here yet and it looks like a winter wonderland." He shoved his hands into the pockets of his Carhartt. "I think today might have been a civil conversation between us. She misses you terribly. Well, we all do." That pang of guilt squeezed at his heart. "There's this woman—a new woman in town. She's teaching Abby and Jacob karate. They're really good at it."

John stood alone in the cemetery and let the bitter cold eat away at him.

"She's really nice." The breeze kicked up and the frozen bits of snow began to circle around him. "I suppose you could say we've been seeing each other. Or better yet we've kissed a few times and want to see each other."

The chill made him ache all over and the sun began to duck behind a cloud dropping the temperature even further.

If this was her sign, he wasn't liking it at all.

"I think it's time for me to move on and find someone. I think maybe that someone is Kym."

The wind whipped up harder and John hunched his shoulders to keep the coat around his neck and ears.

"Heather is worried I'll forget you, but that will never happen. Never. You were the first love of my life and you don't forget that. You're the mother of my children and they adore you."

The wind began to die down.

"I just want to feel again."

The air became still.

"I want to live again. I want my kids to know me as something other than a grumpy old man."

The bitter cold didn't burn through him anymore.

"I want to know you're okay with this."

John stood in silence for a moment. The world around him seemed to settle. And then the sun came out from behind the cloud and warmed up the cold which the wind had kicked up.

He inhaled a deep breath of cold into his lungs. She'd heard his plea and she'd shown him the warmth. This was her way of agreeing with him.

He knelt down again next to his wife's grave. Pressing a kiss to his fingers he then traced them over her name.

"I'll love you forever."

Chapter Fourteen

The door to the school opened as Kym limped across the floor setting up stations for the kids to work. She smiled as she saw Jacob and Abby walk in from the cold.

She stood erect. "Good afternoon." She said and both of the kids stopped, put down their backpacks, and bowed to her. "I have something for each of you."

"Like a present?" Abby asked with her eyes sparkling.

"I suppose you could look at it like that."

Kym walked toward her office slowly and they both followed. On her desk were two uniforms with the name of the school printed across the back.

"You've been such a big help around here I thought you should have a uniform to go with your belt."

Abby snatched hers off the table. "Can I go change into it?"

"Of course."

Abby ran out of the office and toward the changing room, but Jacob stood there with his hands at his side.

"Is there something wrong?" Kym asked trying to read his expressions.

He didn't look at her, but kept his eyes on the uniform. "Are you giving that to me because you're dating my dad?"

Kym hadn't quite been prepared for that.

"No. I have planned to give this to you all along."

He still didn't look up at her. "So you are dating my dad?"

Why hadn't John talked to him about this? It wasn't her responsibility.

"Your father and I have decided we like each other and perhaps we'd like to spend some time together."

He nodded, but his body was still very tense. "I have a mother. She's dead."

Kym could feel her heart clench so tight it had to have stopped beating. "I've only heard good things about her too."

"Would that mean you'll be my mother?"

She stepped toward him. "Jacob, I'll never be your mother. You have one who loved you with all her heart. What I would always like is to be is your friend. And that invitation stands even if things don't work out with your father. I'd always like to be your friend."

He nodded again, but still kept his eyes from hers. "Do I have to wear this?"

She pushed her shoulders back. "You don't like it?"

Finally he looked up at her. "I like it a lot. I don't want to mess it up."

Kym smiled. "You'll outgrow it long before you could possibly mess it up. You earned this uniform, Jacob. I'd be happy if you wore it with great pride."

He moved toward the desk and picked it up. "Thank you, Miss O'Bryne."

"You're most welcome, Mr. Larson."

Jacob held the uniform to his chest. "My dad has been sad for a lot of years. It was nice to see him smile."

He walked out of her office and Kym reached for the back of the chair facing her desk. With just a few words that kid had rocked her from her foundation. Would he always be so accepting?

John watched his son through the front window of the karate school. He was working with Kym's grandfather and he'd never seen eyes so intent.

They were working on some kind of kick. Jacob would execute the kick and the old Korean man would walk up to him, speak with a nod, then step back and the next kick was different—better.

There had been a few pre-school basketball games and one summer of t-ball, but Jacob had never taken to anything before. From feet away, out in the cold, John knew that Jacob had found his calling.

Kym caught his eye and smiled and then she bowed off the floor and disappeared into the back room.

"You're welcome to come inside," her voice came from behind him and he turned to see her standing only a few feet away in flip-flops.

"It's freezing out here."

"That's why you should come inside."

John looked back into the school. "He looks so happy."

"He said the same thing about you."

He turned and narrowed his gaze on her. "He did? When?"

"When I gave him his uniform."

John looked back inside. He hadn't even noticed the uniform. He'd been focused on the happiness in his son's eyes.

"I'll pay you for that."

"I told you, the kids and I have an arrangement."

"It's still your income you're being so generous with."

"I promise to tell you when it becomes a problem," she said with a tightness in her voice. "Go inside and watch your children. It will mean a lot for them to know you saw them."

Kym disappeared around the side of the building from where she'd come and John walked into the school.

The air was muggy from the sweaty kids and the group of parents which gathered around. Immediately there was a need to take off his coat.

"John Larson, your son looks great out there."

He looked down to see Gloria seated in one of the chairs set there for parents—and grandparents.

"Thank you," he said and watched as Kym's grandfather held a pad for him to kick.

"Mr. Kym seems to have taken a liking to him," she said, but John kept watching. "He's been training him for most the class. He's got something special in mind, I can tell."

"You don't say."

Gloria touched his hand and he finally looked away and down at the woman who still wore her nametag from the grocery store pinned to her shirt. "He looks happy, John."

He nodded and then looked up to see the rest of the class lining up for the end of class, but Jacob and Mr. Kym still worked in the corner.

Mr. Kym set the pad aside and came back to Jacob, who bowed. He turned around and knelt down on one knee to fix his belt. When he stood, Mr. Kym was there with a plastic board that he showed Jacob how it would come apart.

John was intrigued.

Mr. Kym then motioned for two older students, who were waiting for class to start, to join him on the floor. The boys bowed onto the floor and then again when they reached Mr. Kym.

With very little instruction the boys stood side by side, each with one leg back and a hand on each end of the plastic board, and waited.

Mr. Kym then spoke softly to Jacob who put his hands up as if he were going to fight.

It was then John realized the board was breakable and Jacob was going to kick through it.

A million little thoughts clouded his mind. First the thought of how exciting it was, shoved out by the fear of failure. With failure came disappointment. Sometimes it came with injury.

Certainly he hadn't been training enough to be kicking boards into two pieces, but Jacobs's leg went back and he slowly lifted it to the board. Mr. Kym nodded. He did the same move again—and again. Then he took an audible breath in and the room went silent as Jacob let out a warrior's cry and kicked right though the plastic board.

John felt light in his heavy work boots and he'd heard himself let out a huge cheer, but everyone else was clapping too.

He noticed Kym looking in his direction. She didn't have a smile on her lips, but her eyes were another story.

This woman had come to his little town when his little boy needed something in his life to make him stand out. Perhaps she'd even saved him—saved them both.

It was the defining moment, he decided. They needed to be together. His family needed her—he needed her.

He felt that sunshine glowing on him again from inside the building as the sky had already begun to grow dark. Abigail knew this woman was sent to him to rebuild. He'd be a fool not to hold on with both hands.

Kym hadn't even seen Jacob break through the plastic board. She was watching the look on his father's face and it had been priceless.

She needed to see that. She needed to know that there was a pride that could surface and take over the man with the crusty exterior.

When he cheered and Jacob smiled at him she thought she might burst into tears and it had taken everything she had not to run to him.

Jacob had remained in protocol, though the smile on his mouth was from ear to ear. He bowed to his board holders and then to her grandfather who had walked slowly to him and placed a hand on each of his shoulders. She could only imagine what he said to Jacob, but the grin remained and her grandfather's eyes gave away his own smile.

Jacob bowed off the floor and ran to his father who scooped him up as if he were a small child and held him tightly.

Those tears weren't just a threat anymore. They were real and they were stinging her eyes.

Her grandfather laid a hand on her arm. "Go, collect yourself. I shall run this class. He will take him home. Tomorrow you can celebrate his triumph."

Kym understood her dismissal, but she wanted to run to him too and scoop him up in her arms. But never would she go against what her grandfather told her.

She bowed off the floor and quietly disappeared from sight.

Chapter Fifteen

Grilled cheese sandwiches shouldn't be a dinner for a growing boy who was celebrating. But Jacob didn't seem to mind the meal as he ate his second one.

John, on the other hand, didn't have an appetite at all.

He'd looked up from hugging his son only to find Kym bowing off the floor and heading upstairs. They had lingered at the school, the kids doing their payment chores, but she'd never come back down. Didn't she want to congratulate Jacob on a job well done?

The kids finished eating and began their after dinner chores which Kym had assigned them. She had a way with people, didn't she? He watched even his two-year-old help in the kitchen. In one night she'd done that voodoo and now his kids suddenly toed the line?

And what kind of ego bash must she have taken to not even stick around and congratulate Jacob on his break? The whole thing wasn't sitting well with him. What was she trying to do—fix a "broken" family? Well, they weren't broken. They were bruised.

There was an ache in his heart that had him literally put his hand to his chest and rub.

"Dad, are you okay?"

He noted the horror in his son's eyes and sat up straight, dropping his hand. "Yeah, just stretching."

Jacob kept an eye on him as he finished his chores.

Cody walked over to him and climbed up on his lap. He rested his head on his shoulder and closed his eyes. The ache in his chest subsided. The unconditional love of his children was better than any medicine.

John rubbed his hand over the curls on Cody's head. Christmas was coming and Cody would be turning three.

The ache was back. Cody's day of birth was a hard day to celebrate. It also was the anniversary of Abigail's death.

He pulled the now sleeping boy closer to him. It couldn't always be a sad day. Cody deserved some happiness on that day even if the sadness of it was etched in John's mind—and heart.

Perhaps he was old enough for a party. It wouldn't be much more than close friends and family. And even perhaps it was time to bury the hatchet all together and make amends with his in-laws.

Jacob sat down at the now cleared off table. "You sure you're okay?" he asked quietly.

"Yeah. Just having a moment."

Jacob nodded. "His birthday is coming. Is that what you were thinking about?"

John felt the sting of tears in his throat, but he wasn't going to let them get any further. He swallowed them back.

"Yeah, that's what I was thinking about."

"We're all going to get through it. Each year will be easier, but we won't forget her."

John fought the tears back harder as they tried to push up. Where did this kid get so much wisdom?

"I was thinking Cody needed a birthday party."

There was a spark that lit behind Jacob's eyes now. "I think he'd really like that." The glimmer quickly faded. "Can we afford that?"

That was another stab into his already guilt ridden heart. "Nothing fancy. Just friends and family." He saw that it confused him too. "Yes, I mean mom's family too."

The glimmer was back, but it was glossy from tears. "I think that would be really nice."

John kissed the top of Cody's head. "You can help me plan it, okay? We'll get busy on it next week after Thanksgiving."

Jacob nodded and stood, pushing his chair in. "Are we going to Grandma and Aunt Heather's for Thanksgiving?"

"Yes you are."

"You're not coming?"

John bit down on his lip. "Not this year. Let's see how the birthday party goes, okay?"

Jacob nodded again and started to walk away, but turned back around. "Are you going to invite Ms. O'Bryne here for our dinner?"

He grit his teeth. "I don't know, kiddo."

"Are you mad at her?"

Perhaps his son had become a bit too insightful. "Why do you ask?"

Jacob shrugged his shoulders and looked down at his feet. "She left after I broke the board. Maybe she was mad."

Oh, she was going to get an earful from him. Now his son was upset too.

"I'm sure she'll tell us," he assured his son, but he knew she would—he was going to make her. She owed his son an apology too.

No woman was going to make an impact and then not be there to help rein in the feelings his kids were having— or him for that matter. Kym O'Bryne wasn't going to ruin his already struggling family. After all, she'd already caused quite a tear in his heart.

Kym hit the floor early the next morning. Her restless night had her needing to kick the heavy bag this morning.

Music blared from her office stereo, this too was unusual. Though she didn't mind music during class to keep the class upbeat, she didn't usually train with it. Training time was to focus and to decompress from everything else around her.

KISS was her music of choice this morning. Her grandfather certainly wouldn't approve of that, but he'd already been picked up by some woman in a Subaru and they were headed to Maggie's for breakfast, he'd informed her.

As she trained, she noticed kids all bundled up, walking down the streets heading to school. Only a few more hours and her school would be filled with those same kids—specifically Jacob and Abby. Kym couldn't wait. She wanted to congratulate Jacob on his break. It was quite a feat for such a new student.

In the mirror she noticed a pickup truck pull up in front of the school and park. It wasn't a truck she recognized so she stopped and watched.

The passenger side door opened and someone stepped out of the truck. She waited to catch a glimpse of the person. Soon enough she noticed the flaming red hair.

Without even bowing off the floor, she ran to the front door of the school as her brother pulled his suitcase out of the back of the truck.

Kym waited with the cold washing over her until he came around the truck and hurried toward her.

Liam set his suitcase on the ground and scooped her up, swinging her around in circles.

"You still look twelve," he said giving her a squeeze before setting her back on her feet.

"I'm thirty. Don't forget that."

"You look wonderful. Is that better?"

"Much. You always were bad with the compliments." She smiled at him. "I've missed you."

"I couldn't wait any longer to get here."

"I don't mind you being early."

Liam picked up his suitcase and set it inside as she shut the door behind them. "Could they have found a more remote location for you? Tell me things are good, or I'm packing you up with Grandfather and taking you with us."

His words stung, but she wasn't going to let him know that. "Things are wonderful. I'll be staying, thank you very much."

"I can't imagine."

"Of course you can't. What do you have? Five hundred students?"

He nodded as his gaze scanned over the small school.

"One floor?"

Kym narrowed her eyes on him. "You've had plenty of schools with only one training floor."

Liam shrugged. "You're right. That wasn't fair." Liam walked further into the school. She knew he was inspecting it. "How old is this building?"

"Sixty years."

"Wow. How do you and Grandfather take care of it?"

The question had her skin itching, which it did when she was put on the spot. "There is a man in town who fixes things when we need it. His kids are students here…"

"Oh, Kym. You're not bartering are you?"

She realized she was fisting her hands at her side. "What does it matter to you what I do here? Things are good. Business is building and Grandfather is healthy."

She knew her brother well enough. He knew he'd upset her and he pulled her to him and held her tightly against him.

"I'm sorry. That wasn't a very good hello."

"I'm not some weak little girl. I was brought up to handle all of this."

"And you're doing a wonderful job." He kissed the top of her head. "No more sister jabs, I promise."

"Thank you."

He backed up from her, keeping her arms in his grasp. "Where is Grandfather?"

Now she smiled. "He's down at the diner. A woman picked him up for breakfast."

Liam laughed and shook his head. "I don't know how he does it. I can't find one woman and the old man always makes out."

"Don't let him hear you call him that."

"I wouldn't think of it. C'mon, show me upstairs."

John sat in his truck by the edge of the lot watching Kym and a man embrace in the school and then walk toward the steps that would take them to her apartment.

He reached toward the heat controls on his dashboard. A little cool air would do him some good. Suddenly he was growing much too warm from the anger that boiled through him.

When he saw the light in Kym's apartment turn on, he backed out of the lot. That was the last straw. He didn't need his children around her—not anymore. She'd hurt them and she'd promised not to. And she'd hurt him too. No woman was worth the feeling that was surging through him.

John drove toward the cemetery. He needed to get this off his chest and only one woman would listen to him and let him tell his side of the story.

The wind had picked up and it had begun to snow as he pulled into the small cemetery. It looked as though they were going to be in for a snowy Thanksgiving.

John pulled over and turned off the truck. The snow was coming down heavier already. He zipped up his coat and pulled a stocking cap out of his glove compartment. Finally he stepped out onto the snow covered ground.

The frozen flowers he'd put on her grave only a few days earlier were peeking out from the snow, but they too already looked as though they'd given up on life.

John stood over Abigail's grave and just looked down. The stone was covered in snow.

The wind grew colder and the sky darker, but he needed to be right there and let it hurt.

"I don't know what is going on. I don't want my children hurt, but damnit, I like her."

He rubbed his hand over his forehead and the image of Abigail ducking into the girls' locker room flashed into his mind. There had been a time in high school when he'd pursued her and she'd given him the slip for a month. Then again before they were married she'd left town for a week to gather her thoughts, she'd said.

"It doesn't sit well with me that there might be a man she didn't tell me about," he said aloud as the snow clouded his view of the town below the ridge. "What if this is some ploy to just get students in her school?"

The temperature dropped and he began to shiver as he shoved his hands into his pockets.

"Am I wrong? Does she need some space?"

The flowers swayed in the wind.

"She'll need me when her grandfather leaves." That much he knew. It would be hard for her to have her family gone. And if the man was still around, well then he'd need to just deal with what he felt for her.

He'd had his heart broken before. It couldn't hurt worse than losing his wife.

Then again he knew it was going to hurt quite a bit. Kym O'Bryne meant more to him than he'd wanted her to.

Chapter Sixteen

Kym had been extremely busy getting her grandfather ready for his trip. Liam had been teaching classes, but she'd noticed that the Larsons hadn't been in class all week.

She hoped everything was okay. It had been snowing for days and that had kept many of her students away from the school. Perhaps the Larsons weren't any different.

John hadn't been in touch with her and she wondered if the holidays were just hard on him. It had crossed her mind many times to call him, but she'd just been so busy.

The email with her grandfather's travel information had come through as she sat in her office listening to her brother lead a black belt class. She clicked the link to print out the information only to find out that the ink cartridge in her printer was dry.

Kym rested her head in her hands. She then looked outside. It had been snowing for nearly three days straight. The thought that she'd have to drive out in the snow didn't thrill her, but she didn't have much of a choice.

She informed her brother that she'd be heading out. She bundled into her coat, pulled on her hat and gloves, and went out into the cold.

Her car was buried under the snow and she scraped off the ice and warmed the car.

The drive into town to Sweet and Salty, the old five and dime, took her nearly thirty minutes. She'd nearly slid off the road three times on her two mile journey.

The store was nearly empty, except for the two married employees who'd owned the store since 1955, as she'd been told on more than one occasion.

Kym quickly found her ink and then strolled through the aisles just in case she found something else she might need.

"Kym?"

The voice was familiar and not the one she would have expected to hear.

"Malory. How are you? What are you doing out in this weather?"

Malory smiled. "We needed diapers and I needed chocolate. But most of all I just needed out of the house."

"How's the baby?"

An unmistakable pride beamed from Malory's eyes. "Oh, she's wonderful. I didn't know I could love anyone so much."

The thought squeezed her heart. She was thirty and had never loved someone that much. Kym wondered what that was like.

"Aren't you teaching?"

Kym shrugged. "My brother is in town. He's been filling in. I've been getting my grandfather packed so he can head back to Ireland and live with my parents."

"Ireland? Wow. That's quite a flight for him, isn't it?"

"My brother will be with him."

Malory smiled. "How is John? I haven't seen him since you visited us in the hospital."

Kym bit the inside of her cheek. "I haven't seen him."

Malory's eyes widened. "You haven't?"

"I'm sure he's been busy," she said smiling, but hurting deep down inside of her.

"Well, this is a hard time of year." Malory moved in closer to her. "Cody's birthday is coming up."

Kym felt the unmistakable feeling of regret take over her body. John was hurting and she hadn't reached out to him. The kids hadn't been in class. How horrible that she hadn't thought of it more. The holiday blues were one thing—she knew Cody's birthday was a whole different reason to be sad.

She needed to make time to go to him—but when?

Malory shifted the small basket she held in the crook of her arm. "When does your grandfather fly out?"

"Two days before Thanksgiving."

"Lots of air traffic. Are you driving him to the airport?"

"Yes. In Grand Junction."

Malory nodded slowly. "I can see if Chris can take you or lend you his truck. That's going to be quite a drive in your car. Perhaps you should head out a little early. Stay in Grand Junction for the night too. This storm has really messed up the roads out of the valley."

Kym hadn't given much thought to that. "I might look into that."

Malory shifted and reached into her purse. "Here. This is Chris's card. It has his cell phone on it. If you need anything or want him to drive you just give us a call."

Kym took the card. "Thank you. I appreciate that."

"Well, I'd better get home. If you see John, tell him to stop by the house. And have a nice Thanksgiving."

"I will. You too."

Kym looked down at the card and then tucked it into her purse. She needed to think about getting a room in Grand Junction. She certainly was going to want to get there in plenty of time and she didn't want to get stuck on her climb out of the valley. Besides, a few days away might do her some good. If she planned it right and took a few days to come home she could enjoy the Colorado winter on her own terms. They usually closed the school during Thanksgiving weekend and that would buy her a few more days to relax and get use to the fact that she'd be totally alone in the town once her brother and grandfather left.

Kym drove back through town, slowly. The roads had iced over and visibility was minimal. She gave thought to calling Christopher and having him drive them to Grand Junction and then again she thought differently. She'd be just fine if they took it slow and easy.

As she sat at the one stoplight between the edge of town and her school, she looked toward the hardware store. Would it hurt just to go in and buy some windshield washer fluid and some ice melt?

Kym turned on her blinker and headed toward the store.

When she pushed open the door to the store she could smell freshly popped popcorn. It only made the appeal of the store that much better.

Kelley looked up from a book she was reading and smiled. "Kym! What are you doing out in this weather?"

"Office supplies ran out. I needed to print my grandfather and brother's boarding passes."

The welcoming look on Kelley's face changed and she narrowed her eyes at Kym. "Brother?"

Kym nodded. "Liam. He came for my grandfather. I didn't expect him until next week, but he came early."

Kelley shook her head. "Red hair? About six foot four?"

"Yes," Kym answered slowly. "Is there something wrong?"

Kelley tucked her book under the counter. "No. Some people in this town are just small minded idiots." She dropped her shoulders. "So, what can I help you with?"

Kym wondered what her comment meant, but it wasn't worth worrying about. Kym understood small towns. She was best to mind her own business.

"I need windshield washer fluid and ice melt."

"You came to the right place."

Kelley helped her with the items she'd come in for. She packed her up an extra big bag of popcorn and Kym was out the door. But not once had she seen John. Truly that had been her reason to stop there. It didn't really matter did it? She'd head out of town in the morning and wouldn't be back until the weekend. If John wanted to talk to her then he would. Kym needed to focus on getting her grandfather packed up.

John waited until Kym had driven out of sight before pulling into the parking lot and trudging into the building.

As soon as he opened the door a paperback romance novel was chucked at his head. Luckily his sister sucked with her aim.

"What the hell is wrong with you?" He bent to pick the book up off the ground.

"You're an idiot."

"Common consensus around here."

"How long has it been since you've talked to Kym?"

He rolled his eyes, set the book on the counter, and shrugged out of his coat. "What does it matter?"

"I asked you a question."

"Since the night she didn't even tell Jacob he'd done a good job in class." He thought about it. He'd gone to talk to her, but then there was that man. "And since she took some guy up to her place."

He realized he hadn't put the book far enough out of reach when she picked it up again and this time, beaned him in the head with it. "God you're stupid!"

John rubbed the spot on his forehead where the binding of the book had hit just over his eye. He wasn't completely surprised to find blood on his fingertips. "What has gotten in to you?"

"That's her brother. Her brother!" She shook her head, walked around the counter, and picked up her book. "You and your stupid head. Did you even consider that?"

"He was coming for their grandfather," he said under his breath.

"Yes. He came in early. And maybe there was a reason she didn't talk to him after class. Maybe something came up. You own your own business. That happens all the time."

John hated being wrong and he hated feeling foolish. So why did it always happen when his heart tumbled after some woman?

He wiped at his forehead again. Apologies didn't come easy either, but it looked like he'd be making one.

Without another word to his sister he started out of the store just as his cell phone rang in his pocket. It didn't bode well that it was Heather calling.

He answered and winced as he heard her voice on the other end. "John! We had a pipe break. You have to come now."

Letting out a deep breath he told her he was on his way and he let go of the thought that Kym deserved that apology. It would hold. The store Abigail had built needed his attention right now.

Chapter Seventeen

The snow continued its assault on the small town. It hadn't taken much convincing on Kym's part for her grandfather and brother to agree to leave early. She'd called ahead and secured a room for the next few days in Grand Junction. With a few phone calls, they cancelled the afternoon's classes and headed out of town with Liam in the driver's seat.

"The climb out of the valley is going to take some time. But I'd bet your trip back in won't be so bad," he said as they slowly drove up the winding road.

"I already decided that I'd come back through Aspen Hills and booked me a spa day too."

"Good. You deserve that."

She was happy he thought so, though she knew she hadn't needed her brother's approval.

The trip to Grand Junction, which usually took an hour, took them three and a half hours to make. Her grandfather had remained calm through the entire drive, but she had finally convinced herself to take a nap instead of holding on to the door handle with a death grip. Someday she'd perfect her grandfather's practiced breathing.

It was dark when they pulled into the parking lot of the hotel she'd booked. Liam helped their grandfather out of the car as she checked in and hurried to open the room.

She'd booked them two rooms. If Liam was going to travel with their grandfather all the way to Ireland he should at least stay in the same room with him for the next few nights—just to remember how Grandfather worked.

The thought gave her slight satisfaction.

~*~

The burst pipe at the florist had taken most of the night to seal off and the rest of the next day to fix. Heather had a mess on her hands and she'd worked right beside him to contain as much of the mess as they could.

"This building is so old," she complained wiping her hand over the back of her forehead. She'd been mopping up water for hours. "Why was this the place she'd had her heart set on?"

John sucked more water off the floor with the shop-vac. "I don't know. But this was where it had to be. I know she'd looked around, but it always came back to this building."

"Every time something like this happens and you and I end up working side by side—I figure she's behind it."

John looked up from his vacuuming and noticed she was leaning her arm on the mop handle and smiling. Her dark curls hanging loose over her eyes.

"She had a sense of humor like that."

"Yes she did," Heather agreed and then began mopping up more water and ringing it into a bucket. "Considering that it's three days before Thanksgiving, I'd suspect she wanted us to get over this petty thing we have going and spend it together."

John turned off the vacuum which was sounding full. "I wouldn't want to ruin the tradition you have with your mom and the kids."

Heather narrowed her eyes on him. She set the mop against the wall. "I can't even say I hate you anymore."

"That's positive."

"I'm trying here, John. Cut me some slack."

"I'm sorry. Go ahead."

"Listen, I've never really hated you. I mean, one look at Cody and you know she would have loved him as much as the other three. I know things just went wrong. I get that."

"But you needed someone to blame."

She didn't come at him with a fist, which was a good sign. "I did. She was all I had."

"No, she wasn't."

He could see her eyes mist up. He didn't like when women did things like that. Why did they always have to cry? The very thought made him tense up and the cut on his forehead from him sister's flying book reminded him he was in foreign territory.

"I miss us being friends. I think three years is long enough to hate each other don't you?"

"I'd agree."

"Good. Then will you please come with the kids to Thanksgiving?"

All John could think about was Kym and wondering what she'd be doing. He knew they'd closed the school early. Kelley had received the call from Kym's brother. It did something very uncomfortable to his chest to think of her alone on Thanksgiving. But, the truth of the matter was she wasn't around and hadn't called and asked him to spend the day with her.

"I'll be there. What should I bring?"

~*~

There had been a truck stop which was serving Thanksgiving dinner all week. Kym, Liam, and their grandfather had their traditional turkey dinner together a few days early.

Of course their family Thanksgivings, in the States, had never been completely traditional. Her mother made

Korean food. Her father made what he could of Irish favorites. She thought she'd been about fifteen before they had turkey, stuffing, and potatoes for dinner.

It made her miss her parents. A few more days around her brother—and not around John—she'd want to fly with them to Ireland. But she wouldn't even consider that. They gave her the school to make her own and she would do that. She just hoped that when she returned, so would Jacob and Abby. She'd missed them—and their father.

Liam handed her a cup of hot chocolate he'd made at the complimentary drink counter in the hotel lobby. Kym held it in her two hands as she looked at the fire crackling in the fire place.

Her brother sat down in the chair next to her.

"You look a little lost in thought."

She smiled. "I was thinking that I miss Mom and Dad. I'm going to miss Grandfather too."

"But you don't want to jump on the plane and head back to Ireland?"

She shook her head. "I think I have too much unfinished business in Aspen Creek."

Carefully, she lifted the cup to her lips. She wondered what John and the kids did for Thanksgiving. Had he sent them to Heather's and he stayed home—alone?

Over the top of her cup she noticed her brother watching her. She locked eyes with him and she knew his Irish wisdom was telling him everything he needed to know and she hadn't spoken a word.

"Tell me about him."

"There is nothing to tell."

He nodded slowly, sipped his hot chocolate, and waited until she couldn't handle it any longer.

"Fine. His name is John Larson. He and his sister own the hardware store. He hung the sign and takes care of the place when something needs fixing."

His eyes widened. "Ah, the man who fixes stuff and his children are your students."

He paid a lot of attention when he wanted to. "Yes."

"How many kids does this man have?"

She swallowed hard. "Four."

Liam ran his tongue over his teeth and sat further back in his chair. "A man with four children? Kym, that's a lot of baggage."

"They're not baggage," she argued. "They are wonderful kids who lost their mother."

"And you've decided that is safe territory to take over?"

"Why are you so…so…irritating about this."

"I'm your brother. If you told me you'd met a nice young man who'd never been married, who didn't have kids, and was a virgin I'd have questions too."

She set her cup on the table. "I'm old enough to take care of myself. And you're younger than I am, so if it were Ian sitting here giving me a hard time I suppose I'd take that better."

"I certainly could arrange that."

"You'll do no such thing. I already have a hard enough time getting through to this man. I don't need my brothers getting in the way."

The corner of Liam's mouth turned up in a crooked grin. "So tell me what's happening with this man, big sister. He hasn't been around this week when I've been there. Is he afraid of your family? Using you for his kids' education? Using you for—something else."

Her skin pricked with heat. "Why are you doing this? I haven't had the pleasantries of your company in a year and in one week you've questioned everything about my life."

"I'm just trying to find out about this mystery man."

"He's no mystery. He's a fine man who has a great family who lost his wife."

"And you're going to step in and fix him?"

"He's not broken."

That smile on his face was getting bigger. "Then why do you want him around? What is it about this man that makes you get so mad over him?"

"Because I love him."

The grin turned into an enormous smile and Liam lifted his cup in salute to her before sipping.

Now tears were stinging her eyes and she wanted to hit her own brother. She didn't want to say aloud, to anyone, that she loved the man who didn't have the decency to come around. He'd pulled his kids from class. He'd all but disappeared and here she was with all these feelings and no way to let them out.

"That wasn't nice." She sat back in her chair and dropped her shoulders.

"Eh, it was the only way I could get you to admit it. Otherwise, no matter how much of a fight you were putting up about being a strong woman—you'd get on that plane with us."

He was right.

She'd said it aloud to more than just herself. Well, now what? She was in Grand Junction and her Grandfather and brother would leave her totally alone when they flew out tomorrow.

It didn't matter. She'd spend tomorrow in Aspen Hills and drive back to Aspen Creek on Thanksgiving. The school wouldn't open again until Monday. She had plenty of time to decide how she wanted to approach John Larson—or forget about their relationship altogether.

Chapter Eighteen

The air was frigid as Kym kissed her grandfather goodbye. He'd never accept a tearful farewell, but Kym wasn't sure she could promise that. In her heart she knew it was the very last time she'd ever see him again and that broke her heart.

"You are a brave and strong woman," he said with a slow nod and his eyes firm on hers. "All children who pass through your school will go on to be strong and brave too." He patted her cheek and moved in to speak in her ear. "Mr. Larson is also brave and strong, but he could be reminded."

That had done it. The tears came quickly and she pulled her grandfather to her. It didn't matter what tradition might have said to do. She loved him and she would miss him and his wisdom.

Her grandfather went on and Liam moved to her. "He's a strong man. I'll bet he has at least another ten or fifteen years in him."

That had made her chuckle as she wiped away her tears.

"You're doing a good job." Liam took her hands in his. "Dad and Mom are very proud of you. When Grandfather gets settled in I'll come back and visit again. I can't wait to see what you build before then."

"You can come back, but you can't change my school."

He kissed her on the cheek. "I wouldn't dream of it."

With that, he was gone too and Kym was alone.

The drive to Aspen Hills was a little easier than the drive they'd had climbing out of the valley above Aspen Creek. She had a massage, facial, and a manicure scheduled for the afternoon. Then, she'd cozy up by the fireplace in her room and think about what she would do with the rest of her life.

~*~

It had been a long time since John had been so nervous. He'd accepted Heather's invitation to Thanksgiving, but he still wasn't sure it was a good idea.

"Dad, we're going to be late," Jacob stood in the kitchen door with his coat on and Cody's gloved hand in his.

"I just don't know if this dessert is good enough."

"They're brownies. They're good enough. Let's go."

John gave him a nod as Abby ran into the kitchen. "Is Miss O'Bryne going too?"

"Why would you ask that?"

"Because she's your girlfriend and you miss her and so do I. I can't find my glove," she continued as she passed through the kitchen and out to the living room.

John shot a glance toward Jacob who was smiling wide. "What was that about?"

"We haven't been to class since that night I broke the board and I told her you were upset with Miss O'Bryne."

"Why would you tell her that?"

"Because you are, but you still like her. You're just upset."

This nonsense about his son being so keen on how he felt was getting old, but it was hard to argue when he was right.

"Listen, I don't even know where Miss O'Bryne is right now."

"Aunt Kelley said she's had a spa day in Aspen Hills yesterday and should be home sometime today."

He was certainly going to have a talk with his sister about filling his son's head with such things. But the comment about her driving home from Aspen Hills had

John looking out the window. The sky was gray, the kind of gray caused by frozen air stirring up a storm. Snow gently fell onto the frozen snow which had yet to melt. He didn't like thinking about her in that car of hers.

One thing was for sure, Kym O'Bryne was a smart woman and if the conditions were bad she wouldn't even try to drive through.

As they loaded up the truck John looked up toward the pass between Aspen Hills and Aspen Creek. The clouds were low-lying enough he couldn't see the top of the mountain. He shook his head and climbed into the truck. He wasn't going to worry about it. He had enough to worry about—he was headed toward his mother-in-law's house and he already had heartburn.

~*~

The hotel room was lonely and Kym couldn't stand to be there one more minute. The conditions outside weren't ideal, but the pass made the route to Aspen Creek a direct drive and if she just took it easy she'd be fine. There was desperation to sleep in her own bed tonight.

As she started out of Aspen Hills, the sun had begun to peek out of the clouds. This is a positive sign, she thought as she carefully took the first turn on the pass.

The overnight snow had accumulated more than she'd realized, but slow and easy and she seemed to be making her way home.

It had been an hour on the road when she noticed that she'd only made it twenty miles. She had another thirty to go and her gas gage was much lower than she thought it should have been.

Around the next turn the sun hadn't been so generous with its heat and the snow on the road was thicker. Her small car grunted along, but it grew slower and slower as she began to crest over the pass.

The thought that it was all downhill from there kept her hopeful, but as she neared the opening that normally would give her the most magnificent view, her car stopped moving and she was stranded in the cold.

For the first time in Kym O'Bryne's life she wasn't prepared.

She surveyed the area around her. About a mile down the road she could see a building. If she was where she thought she was, it would have been the original Rose Family homestead. But honestly, she didn't know where she was.

Kym opened her door and the snow came right up to the ledge of her car. Cautiously she stepped her booted foot out and sunk nearly to her knees.

She reached back into the car and took her cell phone out, which had been charging during the drive. There was minimal signal. She needed to move away from the base of the mountain to get a call through.

Carefully, she took a few more steps, but her footing gave way under her and she found herself face down in a snow bank.

Quickly she pushed herself back up. The temperature was dropping and now she was wet and cold.

Somehow, by the grace of God she presumed, her phone had been protected against her and hadn't suffered.

There were a few more bars now on her screen and she looked in her contacts for Chris Douglas.

John had made it all the way to dessert and so far hadn't been yelled at, called out, or poisoned—or so he thought. Maybe they could make a go of this family thing after all.

Heather brought him a cup of coffee and smiled at him. "It was nice to have you at dinner again."

"Thank you for having me," he said as the doorbell rang.

"Who could that be?" she asked as she set her mug on the table.

John knew who he wanted it to be, but there was no reason for her to even think about showing up there.

"Hey, Chris." He watched as Heather stepped aside and his friend walked through the door, but the perplexed look on his face had John out of his chair. "What's wrong?"

"I got a call from Kym about twenty minutes ago."

His heart slammed into his chest and he hadn't even heard what the man was trying to say yet. In a flash a million things went through his mind and not one of them was good.

"She's stuck up on the pass. That's all I could get. As far as I could tell she's got to be by the Roses' barn."

John swallowed hard and glanced out the window. The snow had been coming down nonstop all day.

"What was she thinking coming across there?" He shifted his eyes to Chris. "Why did she call you?"

His lips tightened. "Because you seem to have disappeared and taken your kids out of her school."

John tightened his jaw. "You sure think you know a lot."

"What I know is there is a woman stranded in a snow storm on the pass. Now, she called me for a reason, but we both know that you're the guy who can maneuver the hill and get her down. So even if you have an issue with her, get your ass in your truck and go get her. Wil says so."

John's mother-in-law walked up behind him and placed her hand on his shoulder. He turned to see her there, her eyes moist.

"Go. You have to get her. Even if you're having problems with her, you have to bring her back safely. Christopher is right. She needs you."

John bit down on his lip. She'd freeze to death in a few hours if he didn't get to her. And yes, he'd been mad that she walked away the other night and he hadn't let the kids go back to class. He'd been torn up about the man she'd taken upstairs, but the cut on his forehead which was now scabbed over, reminded him that he'd been stupid.

"I got a thermos of coffee for her," Heather said as she hurried out of the kitchen. "I'm getting a bag of food too. Mom, get her some clothes. Jacob, go gather all the blankets you can find." She looked up at Chris. "There are two cans of gas in the shed, put them in John's truck. There isn't time for him to go by the store. We need to get him on the road."

He watched as his in-laws hurried about and his children gathered items. It was as if they could all pull together and save Kym from certain catastrophe.

John went to the door and pulled down his Carhartt. He fetched his keys from the pocket as Jacob hurried to him. "We'll be okay with Grandma and Auntie. When you get her down, bring her back here. I'll make her some hot chocolate."

The gesture brought a tear to John's eye and he pulled his son to him and held him tight. "I'll bring her down and she's going to be fine."

"I know," he said pulling back, but his eyes were moist. "She's really strong."

"Right. She's strong."

John stepped into his boots and pulled on his gloves and he hurried out to his truck where Heather was filling the cab with bags of clothes, food, and blankets.

"She's probably scared," she said. "I don't know what she was thinking."

"She probably thought she could fight her way through it. She's usually ready for anything." He smiled as he thought about the day he'd nearly dropped the wrench on her head.

"I like her, John. Don't let this one go." She moved to him, kissed him on the cheek, and then ran back to the house.

"Okay, you have two more cans of gas. Good thing you put the blade on your truck."

John nodded in agreement.

"Do you have a shovel?"

"Yeah, in the back." He opened the truck door. "Chris, thanks. I'll take care of her. Let Wil know."

"I will. And hey," he moved in toward John. "The barn was built to accommodate travelers. Don't be a hero. If you can get her there just stay there. You should get enough signal to call me."

John nodded again and climbed into the truck. Time was of the essence. He hoped she knew not to keep running the car. Did she have enough warmth? God, just let her be okay.

Chapter Nineteen

The heat in the car had begun to dwindle again and Kym wasn't sure she had enough gas to start it again for heat. She'd only stepped outside the car one more time to make sure the exhaust pipe wasn't blocked. The last thing she needed was for Chris to find her dead in her car.

She had enough clothes in her suitcase to change out of the wet ones from when she'd stepped out of the car to make her phone call. But as the sun began to duck behind the mountains, she realized the few dry clothes she had weren't going to keep her warm enough.

Kym closed her eyes and focused on her internal warmth. She made herself see a light starting at her toes. Wiggling her toes she acknowledged that she could still feel them—slightly. The light rose through her body—warming her—reassuring her.

As the light rose into her chest, through her neck, and into her head, she heard a dreadful noise.

She popped open her eyes and there, coming up the road with snow blade against the ground was John's truck.

The joyous feeling had quickly come with frozen tears that couldn't fall. But she could feel them.

John made a few passes to get near her car and then just as a knight in shining armor and a big truck might—he jumped out of the truck and ran for her.

Though her body wanted to do the same and run toward him, she couldn't. Her body wouldn't move. She was paralyzed by the cold which had settled into her, clear down to her bones.

John flung open the door. "Kym, open your eyes. Are you okay?"

She hadn't even realized she'd shut them. With all her might she tried to open them and look into his handsome face. After he called her name a few more times, she managed to get them open.

"Dear Lord, you scared me," he said reaching his hand in and touching her face. "You're frozen. We need to get you into my truck."

Inside her head she thought about helping him, but she couldn't will her body to move. She should be stronger than this. She was a fighter. Why couldn't she even move her legs?

John's arm came around her and the other tucked up under her legs. She felt him lift her from the seat and balance himself in the depth of the snow.

Somewhere, she found the strength to wrap her arm around his neck and hold on as tightly as she could.

John stepped carefully through the snow. Each step he took buried his leg to the knee. He only needed to make it four more steps before the snow wasn't as thick on the area he'd plowed out.

He could feel the cold wet creep into his boots and cake around his pants. But he was focused on getting Kym to the truck. With them both being wet and the sun going down quickly, there was no time to drive back before they'd suffer physically. He needed to get her into the truck and then he needed to head to the Roses' barn.

Her body shook in his arms as he rounded the hood. "Kym, can you pull open the door?"

It was obvious it was taking all her energy to do it, but she managed the door, and he set her on the seat. Heather must have given him every blanket her mother had in the house, but he was grateful as he wrapped them around

Kym. The heater was still running at full blast and he hoped it would begin to thaw her as he walked back to her car.

His boots sunk deeper into the snow. His toes grew colder.

From her car he pulled out her purse, took her phone, and the cord. In the back seat he noticed a pile of clothes. She'd already changed into what she had that was dry. That, he thought, might have saved her life.

As he walked back to his truck his step slipped and John went down into the deep, cold, snow.

Quickly, he stood back up, but his jeans were caked, and his bare hands were now bright red and pained. He'd made sure they packed her more clothes, but he didn't have anything else to change into.

He looked into his truck and saw that her eyes were shut again. The focus wasn't on him. He needed to get her warmed—quickly.

John climbed back into his truck and began carefully turning it around.

"Thank you." The words were so soft he almost thought he'd imagined them.

"You shouldn't have attempted that. You're lucky your phone worked. You're lucky that Chris knew where to find me." He shook his head and looked at her bundled next to him. "I'm just glad you're okay."

He looked at her again and she was crying. What was it with him making women cry? He really didn't think he was that scary. "Are you okay?"

"Cold," she managed. "Sorry," was then next word that slipped through her chattering teeth.

"Well, you might be. The sun is going down and it's about to get really dark. We're going to hole up in the Roses' barn. They built it for the wayward traveler. Trust me you're not the first person to get stuck on this pass."

She wiped her tears on the blanket and turned to look out the window. He'd made her uncomfortable and he didn't want to do that.

The past week of not seeing her had made his disposition less than chipper. Turning her away wasn't what he had in mind. He'd wanted her to explain why she didn't congratulate Jacob on his break. Everything else had just snowballed from there.

But, she was with him now. They were going to be alone in the Roses' barn and cold for at least the next twelve hours. He'd do his best to be pleasant.

John slowly wound his way down the pass toward the road which would take them onto the Rose property. He could see the large two story barn just in front of them—getting there would host its own challenges.

It had been the better part of two decades since he'd been there. One of the Roses he went to school with had held a party there. It had been short lived. You didn't have a party in a landmark like the Roses' barn and think people wouldn't know about it. The thought brought a smile to his lips. When the cops had arrived he and Abigail had run out the back door with half the party. Her hand was grasped in his and they'd run at least a mile before they felt as though they'd escaped. What a night that had been.

The weather had been much nicer. The moon fuller. His heart—well—his heart had been full too, for a young man. There'd been promise in that night at seventeen. If he remembered correctly, it had ended well. Who would have thought all of those moments would be lost?

He looked at Kym next to him and he realized, as he drove to this familiar spot, what they'd started had been full of promise too. A heat rose in his chest when he thought about almost kissing Kym in the back room of the school and then again when he did kiss her in the bakery.

For the first time since he'd met her she looked fragile, much like when she'd held Wil and Chris's baby.

He was male enough to think that was the way she should look—just a little. Perhaps just enough so a man wouldn't be threatened by wanting to take care of her for the rest of her life—or his.

The emotions stuck in his throat as the truck bounced along the road to the barn.

The air was thick with the promise of more snow. The temperature had dropped significantly and the snow beneath them was freezing quickly.

"We're almost there. Are you okay?" he posed the question to Kym whose eyes had closed again.

She weakly nodded and it only brought to his attention that his pants and boots were wet. He needed to get a fire started for both of them.

A few moments later he pulled up in front of the barn. "I'm going to check the doors. Not that a lock will stop me from breaking in."

He jumped out of the truck and went for the door. The snow was deeper there. He'd have to carry her in.

The door had been changed from the time he'd remembered, but he was more than happy to find that the tradition was still *an unlocked door for the weary and stranded traveler.*

John stepped inside. There was a switch next to the door and when he flicked it lights turned on. The corner of the barn had once been a small apartment. There were many legends about that space which he'd heard through the stories of the Roses.

In the livable space, there was a couch and a fireplace. That was exactly what they needed.

He hurried back to the truck and opened Kym's door.

"The snow is very deep here. I'll carry you in."

She nodded her head slowly and he knew he had to get her warm and dry quickly. She was fading on him. If she'd been feeling just right, she'd have carried him inside. He had to wonder if this might be the first time in her life she'd ever needed to rely on someone.

John knew the cold was getting to him as he trudged through the snow with Kym in his arms. She was becoming heavy and that only meant he was fatigued.

As soon as they cleared the door, he hurried her to the couch which was covered with a white sheet. There was no choice but to lay her atop it, bundled in the blankets she had wrapped around her.

Next he needed a fire. He'd brought wood, but as he turned he noticed that there was wood in the fireplace ready to be lit and matches on the mantle. This truly was a place of refuge that the Rose family graciously kept at the ready.

Quickly he went about making up the fire. Once it began to crackle in the old stone fireplace he turned to look at Kym.

Her eyes were open, slightly, but he knew she was warming—he on the other hand was feeling the effects of his cold, wet clothing.

John moved to her, kneeling next to the couch. "I have supplies in the truck. My sister-in-law packed you up warm clothes and I have some water and some food."

A shaky hand moved from under the blanket and Kym rested her cold palm on his cheek. "Thank you. I could have died on that pass." Her voice was soft—weak.

"I'd never let that happen."

"But you're mad at me."

John grit his teeth. Certainly with her lying there he didn't need to get into it.

"I had a moment—a fatherly one. It just didn't play out right in my head." He moved to stand but she rested her hand on his arm.

"Jacob's break. You're mad about it."

John didn't move as he'd planned to. Instead he took a moment to think. "You disappeared. You didn't tell him how good he did."

Kym's eyes closed and then opened slowly. "I'm sorry. I got very emotional over it and my grandfather dismissed me." Her body shook from the cold.

"I should have thought about that," he said taking a moment to tuck the blankets around her tighter. "I'm sorry I didn't let them come back to class."

"I'm proud of him."

"I am too."

"I'll tell him," she said tenderly.

Their eyes were locked onto each other's and the knowledge suddenly washed over him—they were totally alone.

But as her eyes began to drift closed again he knew that they could have a lifetime of tender moments like this if he got her warm and took care of her.

It was then that the cold from his own clothing began to remind him that he too was going to need to get dry and warm or he'd die—or lose anatomy, and he couldn't think of any he'd like to part with.

"I'll be right back."

The temperature must have dropped another fifteen degrees he thought as he opened the door to the barn and stepped out. The snow was now moving in thicker. He could no longer see the Rose house over the crest of the hill and the valley had been absorbed. They were truly alone.

John pulled his phone from his pocket and prayed for at least enough signal to get a call into town. He placed the call to Chris, who he knew would get the message to all the right people.

He could hear Chris's voice, but it wasn't something he could make out clearly so he simply repeated the phrase, "I have her. I have her," until the call was dropped. He'd send a follow up text as well and hopefully it would all be understood.

Pulling down the tailgate he began to gather the supplies his sister-in-law, mother-in-law, and Chris had stocked in his truck.

When he made it to the door with wood, clothes, and more blankets he remembered the thermos of coffee and the bag of food in the cab of the truck.

He moved to the living area and set the pile of items on the floor. Movement caught his eye and he saw Kym sitting up on the couch. That was the best sign so far.

"Can I help you?" she asked.

"One more trip and then I'll need to warm up." He noticed his voice wasn't steady and it was because his body was beginning to shake from being so cold and wet. *One more trip.*

The blast of cold air hit John in the face as he opened the door. His teeth were chattering now and that wasn't good.

He flung open the door to the truck and gathered the thermos and the food. If he didn't get warm soon, he'd be the one needing to be saved.

The barn was already filling with heat, that fact hit his face the moment he walked back inside. It burned against the frozen contrast of his skin.

His grip on the thermos let go and the metal container fell to the ground. Kym sat up full of the life he was used to. A moment later she was in front of him.

"Dear God, John. You're wet and frozen. You came to save me and look at you."

"I—fell on the—pass." Now his words were harder to form. Kym took the bag in his hand and laid it next to the thermos on the ground.

"C'mon. We have to get you out of those clothes."

She pulled him across the room toward the fire where she turned to him.

"Do you have more clothes?" she asked as she began to unzip his coat.

He could only shake his head.

"Okay. Then we need to get you out of these and under those blankets."

There wasn't much he could do as she went to work stripping him out of his wet clothes. Her hands, now warmer, grazed his chest as she unbuttoned his shirt and slipped it off. Just as quickly she pulled a blanket from the couch and wrapped it around his shoulders.

Kneeling down in front of him, she untied his boots and somehow maneuvered them from his feet while helping him balance. It was then he could feel how cold and wet his socks were. He'd be lucky to not lose a toe or two.

Kym went to work on this belt and unbuttoning his pants. This wasn't how he'd envisioned this moment—and he *had* envisioned it.

She slid down his pants—and boxers—leaving him completely naked in front of her, but it didn't seem to faze her at all.

"Lay down." She pressed her hands against his back to lead him to the couch. His muscles protested as they shook.

She took the blankets and cocooned him in them then moved to the pile he'd brought in with more blankets. She threw them all on top of him, including the extra clothes.

His body shivered under the weight of the blankets. Even with the fire only a few feet away he couldn't seem to warm.

Kym began unzipping her coat and letting it fall to the ground, then her sweater, her T-shirt, and when she began unbuttoning her pants he realized he must be cold. She was half naked in front of him and part of him wasn't responding, but his core was warming.

She slid her pants off and stood there in just her socks, underwear, and bra. Every single inch of her was toned and perfect. His mind still worked—that was a good sign.

Walking to the couch she released her bra and it too fell to the floor as her small breasts perked in the cold.

She moved the blankets enough to climb under them and lay her body against John's.

Wrapping her arms around him she rested her cheek to his chest. "Body heat. You need body heat."

"Thank you," he said. His was voice soft as he raised his hand to touch her back and she twitched. From the cold of my touch, he figured.

Her hair was splayed across his skin and he could feel her breath on him.

He'd thought many times of her naked atop him – this wasn't what he had in mind—but much more intimate than the dreams of him taking her in her office, on a dirt road in his truck, or hiding from the kids in his own room. He realized he'd thought it though quite a bit.

Feeling was returning in his body. Nerve endings were coming alive. He could feel her making circles with her finger in the small tuft of hair on his chest. Soft kisses were being pressed against his skin.

Kym rubbed her hands against his chest and his arms. Body heat, he thought, was an amazing fix to many things.

After what had to have been at least an hour, Kym lifted her head and their eyes met. He raised his hands to cup her face. She didn't wince and it meant his body had started to warm. Other parts of him were beginning to warm and he worried she'd be mortified, but he couldn't will them back now.

"I missed you," his voice growled from his throat.

"I'm sorry for whatever I did." Her eyes were sad and he shook his head.

"I'm not used to thinking about anyone but myself—and my kids."

"And I'm use to trying to prove myself." She inched up. Her breasts now pressed against his chest. "I've been thinking about you too much. You have too many people to think about to only think about me."

"But you are all I've been thinking about." He pulled her closer to him so that their faces were only inches apart. "I've only ever told one woman that I loved her." He could see the flash of disappointment in her eyes. "I want you to be the last one I say it to."

Kym's eyes widened and they were deep, emerald green in the firelight. "John…"

"I love you. I couldn't let you wait out this storm up here. When Chris knocked on the door I'd hoped it was you." He pulled her down closer until their lips pressed against each other's. His tongue sought out hers and his hands moved from her faced to roam down her bare back.

She quivered beneath his touch—their cold shivers warmed.

There was no way to hide what he was thinking now—his body was doing the communicating for him.

When she pulled back from him the emerald of her eyes had gone even darker. She moved off of him, standing next to the couch in only her panties and socks, but she didn't let her eyes lose contact with his.

She slipped off her panties and left them on the floor as she climbed back under the blankets, straddling him.

"Tell me again," she said breathlessly.

"Tell you what?" The blood had long drained from his head.

"That thing I'll be the last woman to ever hear."

John grinned up at her. "I love you. Do you love me?"

"I do."

"I won't be easy to love…"

"I want to try," she said easing back onto him and closing her eyes.

Chapter Twenty

John was afraid to move—afraid the moment would end. The fire crackled and gave the dark barn an orange glow.

Kym lay on his chest. Her heart beat heavy with his. The moment they left the barn everything would change. He wondered how he could freeze time.

He lifted his hand and stroked her hair. "Are you warm enough?"

"I've never been warmer," she said on a sigh as she lifted her head to look at him. "I never expected that would happen like that."

He touched her cheek. "I didn't plan this. I swear I didn't."

The corners of her mouth lifted in a satisfied smile. "No, you're not the kind of man to take advantage of a situation like this. You came to save me." The smile grew. "You were mad."

"You shouldn't have tried to drive home."

She pressed a kiss to his chest. "You're still mad."

John hoisted her up so that they were eye to eye. "This changes everything."

"You said that when you kissed me too."

"I mean it. Not only have I only told one other woman I love her, I haven't done this with anyone else." His voice trailed as if perhaps he was embarrassed—and maybe he was, a little.

Kym's eyes diverted for a moment before she lifted them back to meet his. "Am I just the replacement for your wife?"

John sat up slightly and then maneuvered her on the small couch so that she was lying flat on her back and he was looking down at her. "Oh, I didn't mean it like that. No. No, you're not a replacement. Damn. I'm not good at this."

"I thought you were good."

He narrowed his eyes. "I meant it when I told you I love you."

She touched his cheek. "I know you did. I meant it too."

John wiped his hand across his forehead. "I was so cold, how is it I'm sweating now?"

"Because you're nervous." Her tone was calm— peaceful. It quickly crossed his mind that she probably meditated as much as she trained.

"I am nervous."

"Don't be. I'm not going to be all strange with you now. In fact," she lifted to kiss him, "I'd like to do that a few more times."

His body heat was more than rising. "We certainly aren't going anywhere. It's still snowing." He lowered to her and then shot back up. "Oh, shit!"

"What's wrong?"

"Kym, I had no idea this would...I didn't mean to..." He looked down into her confused stare. "We didn't use anything."

That controlled look took over in her eyes. "I take care of myself," she said and he let out a breath.

"I don't mean to make you do that."

Kym looked around the dark barn as if she didn't want to discuss that topic anymore. "What is this place? Are we going to be in trouble for being here?"

John propped himself up on one elbow. "The Rose family was a prominent family in Aspen Creek. This is their barn."

"The big two story one you can see from town?"

He nodded. "That's it. Dr. Rose built it near the pass specifically for his ranch hands to stay in when they were out in the cold. Later, rumor has it, that Lillian Rose's lover lived here."

Her eyes widened. "Lillian Rose? As in the Lillian Rose, actress, Hollywood legend?"

John laughed. "That's her. She's buried in the cemetery even. She grew up in Aspen Creek. I suppose you could say she was the first famous person to bring the elite to the community. But, in time those with more money began to stay in Aspen Hills and Aspen Creek became the quiet spot for them to hide."

"They don't hide too well. I've seen Jessie Charles at Maggie's restaurant."

"Yes you have. Even pop stars move in. Cade used to play professional football and Chris professional hockey."

"That I knew."

"And then some of us just got stuck here." A sadness washed over him. What had he ever done?

"Stuck? You're lucky. You have a foundation. You have roots. I was born in one country, pulled from there and moved to another. I've lived in multiple cities and states. You make a friend only to lose them. You find romance only to leave. You're giving your children stability and purpose. I wouldn't sell yourself short."

He'd never really thought of it that way. Even those who left to do great things came back to where he called home.

"Do you think you can stay in one place? Especially somewhere as small and remote as Aspen Creek?"

Kym looked away and that bothered him. He wasn't sure that if she had to think about it the answer would be the one he was hoping for.

"My brother offered to take me back to Ireland. It would be a chance to be with my grandfather in his last years. I'd have the comfort of my parents around me." She looked back at him and fixed her eyes on his. "I didn't want that. I wanted to make the school work. I wanted to become part of a community on my own terms. I wanted to stay near you."

John rolled himself atop of her, their bodies molding as if they belonged together. "I'll do my best to make that decision the right one."

"I already know it's right."

Sun poured through the windows when Kym opened her eyes after a beautiful night of making love to John. She could feel him breathing steadily behind her, his arm draped over her.

The fire was dying down. She should get up and stoke it back to life. The temperature was dropping.

"Give me a moment to appreciate waking up with you in my arms and then I'll fix the fire," he said as if he'd read her mind.

A few minutes later, John wrapped two of the blankets around himself and fixed the fire. Quickly, he hurried back to her.

"Body heat." He laughed as he pressed his now cold flesh against hers. "It's too bad we even have to leave this spot today."

"I wonder when we'll get this kind of opportunity again."

He didn't answer and she felt him sigh against her. There was no doubt that was her answer. Once their lives were back to normal there wouldn't be time for John and Kym. It would be her and her business. His time would belong to his kids.

A small pang of guilt settled in her stomach. *The kids.* She'd been so wrapped up in what her heart was feeling she didn't think about his kids.

Two people in love usually only thought of each other. But no matter what she was already fifth in line. His kids would always come first. Could she handle that? She'd always had to prove herself, but did she continue to do that at the expense of four kids she adored?

And when two people loved each other they usually wanted to share a life together. But that would mean she'd instantly have four children—if things went that far.

"Are you okay? You're shaking."

She only nodded because she didn't want to look at him. The sting of tears was forcing her to squeeze her eyes shut.

Kym wasn't raised to be anything but grateful—and she was. Grateful that John had run into her at the store. Grateful he'd been the man to hang her sign—fix her furnace—unstick the windows—take Wil to the hospital and then take her to visit. Grateful for the four children she'd already fallen in love with.

But it was Jacob who came to her mind. Would he be grateful for her?

As a student in her school, he thrived. As a big brother, he took his responsibilities very seriously. But as the son of her boyfriend, and maybe someday stepson, would he still accept her?

She thought about the one night she'd gone to their home for dinner. Jacob had been polite, but very cautious. After all, he had a mother and her memory was still fresh in his mind—she knew that.

John pressed a kiss to her neck and suddenly that cloud of doubt began to lift as he slid his hands over her body. She'd consider the possibilities later. Right now she wanted to be the only person for John Larson—for just that moment at least.

An hour later, John started up his truck. The snow had stopped and just as it was in Colorado, the sun was up and warming the snow which had buried them into the barn.

When he walked back into the barn Kym was dressed and folding up all the blankets. A night of passion had put a glow to her skin. Could she possibly be more beautiful?

"The truck is warming. The road looks okay to head down. I'll come back up in a few days and take your car back to town. It'll need a few more days of melt."

Kym only nodded and he knew what she was thinking because he'd been thinking it all night too—what now?

Wrapped in each other's arms in the Roses' barn had been one thing. Back in town where they would have to run their businesses and he'd have to tend to his children—things would be different.

He moved to her, wrapping his arms around her waist and resting his hands on her stomach. She tipped her head back against his chest.

Words crowded his head. *Stay with me tonight. I love you. Go away with me.* Each of them fought for the sentence he would say next, but he didn't know which one was right. He had his kids to think about. His mother and sister would no doubt be waiting there, at his house, waiting for him. Kym had no one—but him.

"Are you ready to go?" He pressed a kiss to her temple.

"No," she sighed. "But that's only because I'm being selfish." She turned in his arms, the blanket still draped over her arm. "It's all going to be different now."

"We'll do our best to not let it be different."

She nodded, but he wondered if she believed him at all. He wondered if he believed it either.

The heater in the truck was working overtime as John eased down the snow-covered, thin, and icy road. Kym admired how he maneuvered the truck with precision. She wondered how long it really would be before he could bring her car down.

She'd been stupid for trying to make the pass in the snow. There would be a time—soon—when she'd need to think about a better vehicle if she was going to really stay in Aspen Creek—and she was staying.

Shifting a glance toward John, she realized she never wanted to leave the small town again—not without him. Just looking at him made her heart swell. But again, the thought that she was not the most important person in his life still stung. How did women do this—move on? How did men?

He'd said he loved her. That wasn't just the cold talking. She was sure of that. He'd meant it. Her heart had tumbled the moment the man crashed into her at the store—even if she wouldn't admit that aloud.

"Do you need to get supplies before you head home?" John asked as they cleared the last turn into town and began to make the drive around the lake.

"No. We had prepared to have my brother a few more days. I should be okay."

He nodded. "I'll get you home."

There was no way to stop the sting of his words. She'd truly hoped he'd take her home with him—already she was asking too much of him, even in her own mind.

Chapter Twenty-One

The small apartment above the karate school was quiet—too quiet.

Her grandfather had taken everything he owned with him and that hadn't been much, but more than she'd expected. How could she feel so alone so quickly?

Hadn't she wanted this her entire adult life? Time to be alone? To be herself? Now she had it and she felt like crawling into a corner and crying.

After making a pot of coffee and changing into warm clothes, that was what she did. An old *Big Bang Theory* played on the TV, but even the jokes were dry and not funny. She wondered if she'd even heard any of them. Her mind was far away. Her mind was focused on John and what he might be doing now.

Because she hadn't had a big meal planned, she didn't even consider the fact that he'd left his Thanksgiving dinner to save her. He'd have to have abandoned his children to someone else to go up the mountain—to have stayed—to have focused only on her.

Kym ran her hand over her stomach where nerves balled. But he'd done just that. He'd left his family to search for her and take care of her. He'd stayed with her—warmed her—loved her.

She closed her eyes tight to stop the tears as she thought of their bodies pressed together. How many times had they made love? She'd lost count, but there was a need for more—more than just sex.

John isn't the kind of man who welcomed change, she thought. No, he seemed like the kind of man who liked routine and since she'd come to town his routine had been disrupted.

He'd altered his work schedule around her sign, around Wil's baby, around his kids coming to her school for karate. Without his wife, things probably had to have been in a certain order for his family. She'd changed that.

And then he'd left his family to rescue her—her who should have known better than to try and drive her tiny car over a snowy mountain. But he'd done it and now she knew he'd done it out of love. He loved her. He'd said so.

Squeezing her eyes shut didn't stop the tears. Why did she feel so abandoned? Because after a night of making love to her and telling her he loved her he'd dropped her off at home and went back to his family—without her.

Kym wiped away the tears with the back of her hand. This was the price she'd pay to love him.

Oh, she could win in any sparring match or save her own life if she were physically attacked, but could she save her heart from the ache it felt now? She wasn't the first person he'd think about every day and she hated being so petty.

Was it supposed to be so hard to love a man?

~*~

Cody's cheeks were already flush with color as John pulled his blanket up over him. He'd been worn out after having spent the night with his grandmother and aunt.

John hoped he had made it clear how thankful he was to them, but they'd only kept asking about Kym.

It was hard to stand there and try to act *normal* about the whole thing. *She's fine. She was cold. The road was too dangerous to get down.* He heard the words over and over in his head. And he wondered if they all saw right through him. Did they know he'd spent the entire night with Kym wrapped in his arms—naked?

There was a burning in the pit of his stomach. He'd told Kym he loved her and that wasn't a lie. He'd never loved anyone but Abigail. He'd never made love to anyone but Abigail. And he'd certainly never left his children wondering where he was to be with a woman before.

John stepped out of Cody's room, closing the door slightly. He walked back to the kitchen where Jacob was still sitting at the table.

"Don't you think you should be heading to bed too?" John asked, noticing the perplexed look on his son's face.

"You didn't come back last night."

John swallowed hard. "No. The roads were pretty bad and the sun was going down. We made it to the Roses' barn and stayed there. We could make a fire there."

Jacob gave him a little nod. "You stayed...together?"

There was a different feeling in the pit of John's stomach now. This wasn't the time to have this conversation with is son, but a good father wouldn't ignore it either.

"We were together, yes."

Jacob looked around the room nervously. "Was there anyone else there?"

"No."

"Are you going to marry Miss O'Bryne?"

John let out a long breath and pulled out a chair. Sitting across from his son he clasped his hands together on the table.

"Why are you asking me that?"

Jacob shrugged. "You know. On TV people spend the night together and sometimes they get married."

"You do understand that we stayed together because it was too dangerous to come home."

"I know. But you like her don't you?"

"I like her a lot."

"Well, if you like her that much are you going to marry her?"

John scooted the chair around toward his son. "What is this about?"

"Grandma and Aunt Heather were talking and they said it's time for you to move on."

That hit him in the chest. *They said that?*

"They said that to you?" he asked Jacob.

"No, I just overheard them." Jacob looked up at him with a panic still darkening his eyes. "Are you going to forget about Mommy?"

A sweat broke out on his forehead and John quickly wiped it away. It would have been much easier had he asked if he'd had sex with Kym.

"Honey, I'll never forget your mommy."

"But if you like Miss O'Bryne and you do marry her she'd be my mommy, right?"

"Sweetheart, your mommy will always be your mommy." He covered his son's hand. "I'll never forget her. I loved her very much and I miss her very much."

"I miss her too and Mason says he doesn't remember her at all."

That broke his heart, but he understood it. Mason had only been two when she'd died. And Cody would never have known her, except for in his heart, John supposed.

"Your mother will live on in us forever, you know that, right?"

He nodded and his forehead crinkled. "I miss having a mom around."

"I'm not good enough?"

Jacob's eyes widened. "I didn't mean that. It's just...well...I'm the only kid in my class who doesn't live with his mother."

"Your situation is special."

"I don't like my situation," he said. "I just want you to know I like Miss O'Bryne and if you wanted to marry her it would be okay. And I still miss Mommy."

John pulled Jacob out of his chair and into his arms. Alone in the kitchen his son didn't pull away.

"I think we're doing okay," he said as he gave Jacob an extra squeeze and then pulled back to look at him. "But I do like Miss O'Bryne a lot."

"A whole lot?"

"A whole lot." He smiled as he said it.

"You kissed her the other night when she ate dinner here."

"You saw that, huh?"

Jacob nodded. "Did you kiss her again?"

Now John could feel the heat under the rim of his shirt collar. "Yes, I've kissed her a few times."

"Do you like it?"

John bit down on his cheek before answering. "I do."

He could see the dimple now form in his son's cheek. "Did you kiss her when you were alone in the barn on the hill."

John narrowed his eyes. "Why don't you go to bed?"

Jacob's grin widened. "Can I go back to class on Monday?"

"Yes."

"Good." Jacob pushed back his chair and stood. "At least if you marry her or keep kissing her I can go to class."

John ran his hand over his hair, well how could he possibly let his son down. He might not be ready for marriage…but he could take a few more of those kisses.

~*~

Saturday morning was still too quiet as Kym woke much later than she normally would. Saturdays were made for early morning training so the occasional day off should have been a real treat.

But she was lonely.

The sun was up and when she looked at her phone on the nightstand she was more than surprised to find that it was past nine in the morning.

When was the last time she'd ever slept that late?

Yesterday, she thought, when she'd awaken in John's arms before making love to him again.

As she pushed back her blankets she heard a noise outside. Something was hitting her window.

Quickly she swung her legs over the side of the bed and ran through the small apartment. John had thrown pebbles at her window once—could that be him?

Kym flung open the curtains and looked down below. It wasn't John. Instead there stood Jacob, Abby, Mason, and even Cody.

She opened the patio door and took a step out onto the small patio, into the bitter chill of the morning.

"What are you four doing here?" The smile on her mouth pushed at her cheeks.

"Mrs. Maggie is saving us the big booth for a late breakfast," Jacob said. "Would you come have breakfast with us?"

"Just the four of you?" she asked on a laugh.

Four sets of eyes looked toward the corner of the building where she could see John leaning against the wall a grin on his lips.

Her heart flipped in her chest. "Mr. Larson, did you send your children to ask for a date?"

"Not much of a date with four kids," she said, his eyes still cool as he watched her.

"I'd love to have breakfast with you all. I still need to get dressed." She shivered from the cold that blew through the canyon. "Here," she said turning back into the apartment and taking her keys from the counter. She walked back to the patio. "I'm sending down the keys. You can open the door to the school and I'll be down in a few minutes."

She dangled the keys for a moment. "Step back. I don't want them to hit you. Just let them fall on the snow," she said and all of the kids stepped back.

When Jacob had them in his hand, she gave them a wave and hurried back to the bedroom to get ready.

As she searched through her drawers she also brushed her teeth. After rinsing away the toothpaste, she began pulling a brush through her hair.

She spun out of the bathroom and nearly screamed aloud when she saw John standing in her bedroom door leaned up against the door jamb casually, just as he'd been outside against the side of the building.

"Dear Lord, you scared me."

"The kids are kicking things downstairs. I hope that's okay."

"Of course."

"Good," he said standing up straight and moving toward her. "I missed you so much I had to come see you."

"You missed me?" she asked as he wrapped his hands around her waist.

"Jacob says I can keep kissing you."

She opened her eyes wide. "He knows what we did?" She could feel the heat rise in her cheeks.

"He says people who spend the night together on TV eventually get married."

Kym pressed a hand to her chest. "Oh, what does that really mean?"

"It means he's so innocent and he watches too much TV." He lowered his mouth to hers and consumed those thoughts that had begun running through her head.

When he pulled back he looked at her. "This is where it gets complicated. I can't curl up with you in your bed. I can't invite you to stay in mine. And when I come asking you to share a meal with me I bring an army."

"I love your kids."

"They seem to be very fond of you as well."

"You missed me?" She repeated his statement from earlier which had stuck in her head.

"I said I did, didn't I?"

Kym nodded. "I just needed to clarify because I was missing you all night."

He ran his hand over her hair. "We can make this work. It's just going to take some dancing around."

"I get that. I'm willing to do that to be with you." She wrapped her arms around his neck. "I'm a very patient woman."

"I'm not a very patient man."

"I suppose we could both learn something from the other."

"Well, I want to learn how you order your eggs. I'm starving. Let's go."

Chapter Twenty-Two

Maggie had in fact saved them a booth in the restaurant with a hand drawn sign that said RESERVED. Kym smiled wide when she saw it.

"You must be pretty important in this town," she said to John as she slid into the booth next to Mason.

"I've been known to fix a thing or two for a few people."

"Something tells me it's much more than that."

Maggie walked toward the table with a smile. "Family outing I see."

The words made Kym slightly uncomfortable. *Family.* But she wasn't part of their family. She was very much alone in the town now. Kym shifted a glance around the restaurant. There were many families seated there.

"Mason was hungry for Maggie pancakes this morning. I couldn't disappoint him."

"We can get him all fixed up then," Maggie said and then turned to Kym. "I'm glad to hear you're safe too. That pass is very tricky in this kind of weather."

Kym opened her mouth to speak, but Cody tugged on Maggie's apron and diverted her attention. "Pancake."

"You too?" Maggie lowered her forehead to his. "I'll make it special for you."

Maggie took the rest of the orders and hurried away.

John reached across the table and rested his hand on Kym's. "Are you okay?"

"Does everyone know I was stupid enough to try and come down that pass?" she asked quietly.

"No one thinks that."

She lifted her eyes to meet his. "I could have died up there," she said with her voice hushed as much for those around her as for the kids.

"But you didn't."

Maggie returned with coffee and juice. Kym sat back in the booth and occupied herself by coloring a picture with Abby.

John hadn't liked how Kym closed up after Maggie had mentioned the pass. Hell, he'd gotten stuck up there more than once—though not as desperately as she had where they had to take shelter.

He noticed how uncomfortable it had made her when Maggie lumped them together as a family too. Well wasn't that logically the next step? They had kissed, made love, and told each other they loved one another. It should make her jumpy when people included her in their family.

John looked around. A few heads gave him a nod and then went back to their conversations and meals. He'd thought bringing her along to breakfast wasn't a big deal. However, it hadn't occurred to him that it would be their first time out together. They'd never been in public as a couple and here she was coloring with his daughter. Oh, people were going to talk. That shouldn't bother him. He'd been gossiped about before. But it bothered him because this wasn't fodder for gossip. This was Kym's life—his life.

It wasn't long before Maggie served them and his kids began to move plates back and forth so that their food could be cut. Kym dove right in and began to help, but it must have been overwhelming to not have had a moment to herself to even sip her coffee.

What had he been thinking? This was such a mistake. This was only their second meal together with the kids and it was always such chaos.

Once the kids were settled and Kym was able to begin eating, he watched her. This was something he could get used to.

"What do you have planned today?" he asked as she took a bite of her pancakes.

"I'll need to spend some time working on lessons."

"Isn't it always the same?"

Kym looked up from her plate and chewed her bite slowly. "Is every furnace filter the same?"

"You have to adjust."

"Same with lesson plans in martial arts."

Jacob wiped his mouth and set his napkin back in his lap. "Will you train today too?"

"Privately. I always train a minimum of an hour a day."

He pursed his lips and his forehead crinkled as he thought. "Could I train with you? I could do extra jobs at the school," he added quickly. "I know I'm not just getting lessons since you and Dad are dating."

John clamped his teeth around his fork and shot Jacob a look.

Kym turned her attention to him fully. "You'd like to train on Saturday when the school is closed? I won't have a class of students."

"I'd like to, but only if you said it was okay."

Her eyes were soft and the corner of her mouth lifted. "Jacob, I would enjoy some company."

The smile on his face brightened into his eyes. "Thank you, ma'am."

"You graduate next week. Perhaps you'd like to learn your next form."

His eyes grew wide. "Yes. I would."

"After breakfast, and only if your father doesn't have anything for you to do at home."

Jacob looked at his father now with pleading eyes.

John sipped his coffee before looking at Kym. "This is a day off for you."

"And I will be training. He's asked to train more and with me."

"Are you saying this is fine?"

"I think that was what I said."

"He can pay you off with more chores?"

Kym set her fork down and placed her hands in her lap. Her eyes were focused on him directly. "Do you have a problem with me working with him?"

"I just don't want you to feel obligated."

"I'm capable of telling him no if it wasn't going to work for me."

"Fine. I'll bring him by. But you have to bring him home."

"Fine, but I don't have my car."

He nodded. "You will. Chris and I will head up and bring it down in a few hours."

"Thank you," she said softly and smiled.

"We're having lasagna for dinner."

"Sounds nice."

"You'll be staying." He narrowed his eyes to her.

"You should come to class," she said picking up her fork. "You could learn some discipline and manners—such as how to ask a lady to dinner."

He smiled. "You'll be there?"

"Of course I will."

~*~

Kym hadn't planned to have anyone in the school with her today, but Jacob had a buzzing energy that was affecting her too.

"I'm glad you came to train with me, but I also have to work on my form. I have a competition next week and…"

"Competition?" His eyes grew wide. "You're going to compete like in a tournament?"

She smiled. "Yes. I'm going to judge too."

"That is so cool."

"I'll be judging the sparring. That takes focus."

His mouth had dropped open and his eyes grew even wider. "Can I compete?"

Kym felt her own smile shift. "Well…um…do you think you're ready? You'd only be able to compete among your belt ranking and age, but…I don't know if…"

"Oh, please. I'm ready. I know my form very well. I'll show you." And that was what he did. He started in a ready stance and began his form with the precision she'd seen her brothers have when they did the form.

Had she been judging him, he'd have a near perfect score and she had to assume she was watching with a very critical eye.

When he was done, he came back to ready and then bowed to her.

"I'm ready," he beamed and she couldn't disagree.

Her heart began to pound in her chest. This wasn't her decision and she knew that.

"Tonight over dinner we'll talk to your father about it."

"Thank you."

"By the way, Jacob. I owe you an apology."

His eyebrows came together in a look of confusion.

She reached her hand out and touched his shoulder. "I didn't tell you how proud I was of your break the other day." She felt his shoulders stiffen under her hand. "I got very emotional and my grandfather dismissed me from the floor."

That had his eyes opening wide. "He did?"

"It might have shown weakness to the other students. But I'm afraid it was misread by your father and I'm afraid perhaps you thought I wasn't happy for you."

He shrugged and she knew that was her answer.

"You've learned so much and you've become very strong. I'm very proud of the student you are as well as the young man.'

Jacob smiled, she thought perhaps unwillingly, but it was genuine and he couldn't have hid it if he tried.

"Are you ready to train more today?"

He gave her an enthusiastic nod. "I'll work over here so I'm not in your way."

He moved over to the side of the floor and turned away from her. Again, with the same discipline and precision he began to work on his form.

Kym took a deep breath. She wanted him to compete. Knowing how to win—or lose—was an important skill. Getting up in front of strangers and overtaking your fear with confidence was something every third grader should master.

She wondered if John would let her take him. With all the things that had happened in his life it could be a very fragile thing to push him into the competitive world—or it could be the one thing to push him onward to be great.

Either way she was sure she'd need to be prepared when they brought it up to him.

Chapter Twenty-Three

From the moment Kym and Jacob had discussed the competition; she'd practiced in her head what she'd say to John.

She'd never anticipated that the moment they sat down for dinner Jacob would lead with, "Miss O'Bryne is doing a competition and I want to go too. She said I could and I want to go. Okay, Dad?"

The air whooshed out of her lungs and she saw John's eyes widen and a cloud of what she'd only be able to explain as fury hazed them.

"She did, did she?" He was glaring at her. This wasn't how it was supposed to work.

"I said we'd discuss it with you." She shifted her eyes to give Jacob a firm look which had him lowering his head and focusing on his dinner. "But perhaps we'll discuss it when the meal is over and it is only the three of us."

There was no need to talk about it while the others were at the table and she could already see that John wasn't happy. Perhaps it was how it was brought to light and she wouldn't blame him for being upset. She couldn't blame Jacob for being so excited either.

When the meal, which had been too quiet and too tense, was over the three younger children went about doing their chores and then they were off to watch TV before their baths.

Kym moved toward John at the sink where he was washing dishes. "Let me do this and you go sit with Jacob."

"Doesn't seem like there is anything to discuss. From the sounds of it you've done all the parenting on this."

Kym grit her teeth. "He's very excited and what he said wasn't necessarily the way he and I had discussed it. I'd never take over the parenting of your kids."

The vein at John's temple pulsed and the grip he had on the glass in his hand could only spell disaster if he squeezed it any harder.

She reached out and touched his arm. "Give him just a moment of your time. I can leave if it's necessary."

He turned and gave her a glare. "I'm not asking you to leave."

"And I'm asking you to take a moment and let your son speak to you. I don't care if you tell him yes or no, just listen to him."

The anger in his eyes seemed to soften and he handed her the glass and the rag.

John turned and walked back to the table. He took the chair, spun it around, and sat facing his son with his arms over the back of the chair he now straddled.

"Tell me about the competition."

Jacob began telling him in great detail what Kym had told him about the competition. He explained how he'd only get to do one form, but there would be lots of people there doing other forms, breaking, and sparring.

"Miss O'Bryne is competing in forms and she's judging sparring which I can do when I'm older. I can't spar yet, though she said someday she'd let me put on her gear so I know what it's like."

Kym kept her back turned from them and finished the dishes. A smile permeated her lips listening to Jacob talk so quickly.

"How much will this cost me?" John asked.

Kym turned off the water and faced them. "As it happens I have two invitations to the tournament. One was for my grandfather, but of course he wasn't going to compete. So that leaves an entry open."

"You're saying it won't cost me?"

"This time. Tournaments aren't always free. This was an invitation sent to the school and the entry fee waived was also a gift for me to judge."

John nodded. "That was nice."

"Very nice. So this time," she reiterated, "it won't cost."

"And when is it?"

"The second Saturday of December."

She watched both John and Jacob drop their shoulders and it was as if the room had deflated around her.

"Never mind, Dad. I won't go." Jacob stood from the table and left the kitchen.

Kym watched as John ran his hand over his forehead. His eyes had gone sad now.

"What just happened?" Kym asked with the dish towel in her hands.

He didn't look at her. "That's Cody's birthday."

She knew enough to mean that it was the anniversary of Abigail's death and she saw what that did to him.

"I didn't know."

He nodded. "I know. There will be others, right?"

"Always. And he's amazing so he'll have the chance again, and…"

"Thanks." John cut her off and stood. He pushed in his chair. "I should get their baths ready."

Kym pushed back her shoulders. "I should probably be going then."

There was a piercing in her chest that she couldn't will away.

She draped the towel over the sink and headed toward the door to pick up her coat.

"Thank you for letting me eat dinner with you," she said as she passed through the living room where the three younger children watched a movie.

"Bye," they all said in unison, but she noticed Jacob wasn't there.

That was fine. She'd talk to him tomorrow.

She pulled her keys out of her pocket and headed out to her car. A moment later she heard the screen door slam and John was following her.

"You're just leaving like that?"

"I'm in the way. You invited me to dinner and now I'm in the way."

"Dear God, what am I supposed to do?"

"I don't know. Thank you for a nice meal and time with your son." She opened the car door and he reached for her arm.

"There's a lot going on here. What made you so mad?"

"Mad?" Was she mad? No she was hurt. Tears were stinging her eyes and she realized she was throwing a fit. A little girl fit. "I'm not mad. I'm hurt. I need to go."

She broke from his touch, climbed into the car, and drove away. She loved him. She loved him so much and yet she'd never be the only one. This time she knew it wasn't about the kids. Fine, she'd always come after the kids, but she'd never come after the memory of Abigail and she couldn't live with that.

John raked his fingers through his hair. What the hell had that all been about? He hadn't missed the drama that women brought to a man's live no matter how much he missed his wife. Heather and his mother-in-law had given him enough drama over the years and now he'd invited more in.

Who did she think she was to just run out like that? What had he said? What did he do?

He ran his hand over his face and then he realized what had transpired. Kym was smart enough to know that Cody's birthday wasn't the happiest of dates in their world. Though they were going to do everything they could to combat that, he hadn't reacted too well and neither had Jacob.

Crap, it could wait until tomorrow and he'd go to her. He'd get it all out in the open and they'd talk.

On a breath he took his cell phone out of his pocket and dialed his sister.

"Can you come over and do baths and get these guys into bed? I need to do something." When she agreed he slid the phone back into his pocket. Suddenly, it wouldn't wait until tomorrow.

~*~

Tears rolled down Kym's cheeks and she hated it. When had she gone so soft? Never—and she knew it had been never—had she cried over a man. This was ridiculous.

She'd taken a few moments to kick the heavy bag in the corner. Then she set up the board and broke through it. Once her frustrated energy had been spent, she dragged herself upstairs to finish the pity party with a glass of wine. She could do that now. She was a thirty-year-old adult woman who didn't have anyone looking over her shoulder anymore.

Kym filled the wine glass nearly full, corked the bottle, and leaned against the counter.

This was a speed bump in the road, she thought. After all she was a grown woman who could deal with her feelings. She could kick, punch, and break things. She could wash it away with wine. And then tomorrow she could talk to John rationally.

Again, he'd done nothing at all wrong, it was her own feelings that had been hurt and now she looked like an idiot.

With a long indulgent drink she swallowed the wine and it went straight to her head. This wasn't much like her, but it felt good to let go just a bit. There would be no students until Monday. Alone in her house it was okay if she got just the slightest bit drunk—which with one long drink of wine she was already doing.

It didn't take long and the glass was empty. Kym blinked hard and decided she was going to fill it back up.

She did just that. Another sip and she realized she was already nearly drunk. It might have been the first time she'd felt quite like this. Hadn't she ever just let it all go? Just stopped being so proper and trained to do everything in just the right way?

It seemed as though John Larson was teaching her quite a lesson now.

Kym strolled to her sofa and clicked on the TV. She kicked her feet up on the table and laughed. She was drunk in the solitude of her own home and she was putting her feet on the furniture. There was a wicked moment when she thought about running across the training floor downstairs with her shoes on—without bowing.

She laughed. Pity parties could be a little fun, she thought.

Then she heard knocking.

She looked around. It was the door downstairs. Who would knock on the door downstairs on a Saturday night at, she tried to focus on the clock across the room, but it was fuzzy, well in the dark at least.

Kym stood, set her glass on the table, steadied herself and started down the steps.

As she cleared the hallway that lead to the school she looked at the training floor and thought about running across it—but even drunk she had some respect.

She walked around it and could see the shadow of a man near the door. What did he want? Why would—then she saw his face.

Kym unlocked the door and pulled it open. "What are you doing here? You have kids at home."

"Right, with my sister. Now let's go upstairs so we can talk."

"We don't need to talk. I've had me a little pity party and I'm done."

He was looking at her now with a critical eye. "Are you drunk?"

"I might be. I've never been drunk before and if this is it then yes I am."

"Hmm," he purred looking at her through narrowed eyes. "You've never been drunk before? And you chose tonight to do it? By yourself?"

"I'm an adult. I don't have anyone looking over my shoulder and I don't have to answer to anyone—anymore. Especially you, John Larson. I can drink as much wine as I want and kick my feet up onto the table *and* I can rot my brain all night long with television. I think I might even have some chocolate stashed somewhere in a cupboard. Ice cream. I should walk down to the store and get some ice cream."

John pressed a hand to her mouth. "Dear Lord, shut up."

Kym simply stared at him while he pressed a hand to her mouth.

"You're making me want to drink now," he said lowering his hand and holding up a finger. "Don't say another word."

Kym nodded.

"I should come back tomorrow. You're in no condition to talk rationally to me."

"I'm not rational. I'm dumb." She threw her arms up in the air and started back to the steps that led up to her apartment.

John shook his head. What in the world had gotten into her? He turned and locked the door then followed her up to her apartment.

By the time he'd reached her she'd sunk onto the couch with a full glass of wine in her hand and her feet up on the table.

"This is the life huh?" He wanted to smile, but he refrained.

"Why are you here?" She drank back the wine and then let out a long breath.

"You were upset and I wasn't sure what I did. I'm not good at all with this relationship stuff."

"You were married. You know how a woman thinks."

"Maybe." He walked toward the couch and took a seat on the other end. "Abigail had her share of fits and we did enough fighting to last me until I'm good and old."

"And you loved her," she said softly.

"Of course I did." He stood and paced in a circle. "What the hell was that about?"

"Nothing." She wiped at tears that were now freely falling down her cheeks. "I told you I'm having a pity party and you're interrupting it."

"A pity party over what?"

"I'll never be the first woman you loved. And you still love her because she didn't leave you in a fight. She died. It's different than if you'd gotten a divorce. She died and you still love her."

John felt the air grow heavy in his lungs and he realized he was holding his breath.

"You're mad at me for loving my wife?" he asked softly.

"I told you," she held up a finger. "I told you I was having a pity party. A very unreasonable one at that."

"You could say that again."

Anger drummed in his head, but it only fringed on what was in his heart. No matter how incoherent she was right now, she made some sense. If he sat down and had a decent conversation with her, whether she was drunk or not, maybe he could explain how he felt. Then again, he was really bad at this part.

Kym drank the rest of the wine, stood, teetered, and then headed to the kitchen.

John followed her and as she lifted the bottle of wine, he stopped her. "I'm all for getting drunk and mad. I've done it myself enough to know what you're going to feel in the morning too. But let's talk."

"I'm being foolish and stupid. Now I'm embarrassed that you're seeing me cry. I don't cry."

"I've seen you cry."

She looked up at him with red swollen eyes. "I know. And I don't cry, but I cry over you."

John cupped her face in his hands. "And why is that?"

"Because, I love you."

He smiled and pressed a soft kiss to her lips. "And I told you that I love you too. So why are you doing this to yourself?"

"I want to be special. I've always been the girl in this world run by men—my job," she clarified. "I've been the only daughter. I've been the little one. The unimportant one…"

"I don't think that's true."

"It's just," she let out a breath. "You've known true love before and I haven't. Will you always think of her? Will the kids hate me in the end because I'm not their mother?" She pressed her hands to both sides of her head and he knew her head was spinning.

"They'd never do that."

"I know." She wiped away more tears. "This is all foolish, but it's how I feel."

John pressed another kiss to her lips. "How can I make you understand how important you are to me? How can I prove to you that it's you that I love?"

"Just hold me." She hiccupped. "Let me finish this stupid pity party. Tomorrow is a new day. I'll be fine."

He laughed as he pulled her into his arms. "Oh, no you won't."

She laughed too and then winced. "You should go home."

"No. I'm going to stay with you."

Kym looked up at him, her eyes wide. "Here?"

"Kelley has things under control. I have a need for you. A need to hold you all night."

She moistened her lips a couple of times. "Only hold me?"

He let a smile form on his lips. "You're drunk."

"Not that much. I won't say no if you want to make love to me." Her words swayed with her body.

"I want to."

"Then carry me to bed if you're mine all night."

He scooped her up into his arms.

"John," she said softly as she pressed a kiss to his neck.

"What?"

"I'm sorry I threw a pity party."

"You're entitled," he explained as he skirted the coffee table by the couch.

"Will you love me forever? I mean, even if you love her, will you love me from here on out?"

"That is a promise I can make."

Chapter Twenty-Four

There were only three days until the competition and Kym had never worked so hard on a form in her life. For some reason there was a need to make this one really count. Was it for her father? Or her grandfather? Did she need it to prove that she could compete against others in this male run industry?

Or was it for herself since she'd been so foolish.

The night of drinking wine and sobbing had ended well enough—John was in her bed wrapped around her and he'd made sure he came back a few more times when it was convenient. Jacob had been joining her on Wednesdays and Sundays to train, even though he wasn't going with her.

They'd talked about the birthday party they were going to have for Cody and she was most sorry she'd miss it. They should celebrate his joyous life with family and Jacob had told her that was going to include Abigail's family.

All the better she thought, that she'd be in Grand Junction for the weekend. Let them all bond and she'd kick the crap out of the competition—figuratively speaking.

The morning of the competition Kym loaded up her car. She wasn't going to take any chances so she packed extra food, extra clothes, and made sure she had John teach her how to put chains on her tires.

The sun was just peeking over the mountain peaks and it shimmered off the lake. Kym took it all in. What a beautiful day.

The competition wasn't until noon, but she had a few other items on her agenda before she left town.

She drove to John's house and parked down the street. It was a quiet day for them and she wasn't going to be responsible for waking anyone so she walked up quietly to the house.

She'd bought a gift for Cody and left it on the doorstep. She couldn't wait to hear about the party.

As she drove out of town, she stopped by Maggie's and got a breakfast sandwich and a cup of coffee.

Maggie's husband, Harvey Wilson, sat at the counter. "Looks like you're headed out of town early."

Kym smiled. "Yes. I have a competition in Grand Junction."

Maggie handed her the bag with her food and a Styrofoam cup of coffee. "You drive careful. And if you don't think you can make it back..."

"I won't even try it."

She gave her a nod and a smile as she left the restaurant and headed toward her next destination.

Kym pulled through the front of the cemetery and down the small roads which lined it. Before she'd left home she made sure to find the plot she was looking for. There was no time to spend all day wandering a cemetery even if it was filled with some very famous people.

She stopped her car and parked at the marker she'd been looking for. The headstone was easy enough to find with a bouquet of candy cane flowers.

LARSON

Kym let out a long breath and walked to the stone.

She set the flowers down that Heather had made up for her the night before.

"Hello, Abigail. My name is Kym O'Bryne and I'm in love with your husband." She chuckled when she thought of what it was she was doing. "Your children are wonderful and I would give anything to help John raise them in your absence. But, I felt as though I should come by and let you know I never intend to replace you. But he says he loves me and I love him, though I'll never be you."

She thought she'd cry. She'd even given herself permission to do so, but the tears weren't there.

The sun had fully crested over the mountain now and the air warmed.

"If he'll let me, I'll take care of him for the rest of my life—and the kids. But I needed you to know that he loves you and I know he always will."

A warm breeze blew through the cemetery on the chilled December morning and it hit her enough that she sucked in a breath and she could smell the flowers.

Kym felt as though she'd done what she needed to do. Three years to the day after a woman she'd never known had died; she'd made her peace with that woman. But in her heart she felt as though she had her permission to love him—them.

Kym had signed in at the tournament and been instructed as to what was expected of her as a competitor and a judge.

She wasn't unfamiliar with tournaments, but each one was just a bit different. And this one was the first one without her family.

Texts had come from both of her brothers wishing her well. An email from her parents had done the same. But it was the email from her grandfather that had put the feeling of accomplishment in her heart.

Competition was first and they would start with black belts and work their way down from there. When her ring assignment was called Kym walked over and reminded herself, continuously, to breathe.

She was the fourth competitor in the ring and her competition thus far had been steep. There were three more to go after her so she had to make it count.

Kym gave her presentation and then took a deep cleansing breath and began her form.

Muscle memory had kicked in and her body moved in the way it had been trained to. Each block was sharp—each punch, strong. Her breath was loud and her cries of confidence—the same.

Each kick was higher than she'd ever kicked and the form was the best she'd ever done. As she bowed to the judges when it was over she thought she'd never performed as well—and no one from her family had seen it.

She turned down on one knee and the judges scored. She listened as they called them off. Each score was higher than the other judge and higher than her competitors. So far, she was in first place.

There were no cheers or applause. It was on to the next competitor and the next.

When they were finished the judges and the scorekeeper convened in the center of the ring. The competitors, four men and two women, were asked to stand.

The announcer announced the third place winner and it wasn't her. He announced the second place winner and it wasn't her. She held her breath as she felt the eyes of the man next to her on her. When the announcer announced the first place champion she heard it.

"Miss Kym O'Bryne from O'Bryne Karate in Aspen Creek, Colorado."

The smile erupted on her lips before she could pull it back and control it. She walked to the head judge and accepted her trophy, but then she heard it. There was applause and whistles and cheering. She heard her name and she looked around.

To the side of the ring there stood John with Cody on his hip. Mason was on Kelley's hip and Abby and Jacob stood next to Heather and their grandmother in their uniforms.

She hadn't cried when she'd visited Abigail, but the tears were there now.

She bowed to the head judge and then as a group to the head table where grand masters sat before she made her way to the family—John's family—her family.

"What are you doing here?" she asked as Jacob bowed and then gave her a hug.

"We didn't want to miss you," he said to her.

"You're in uniform."

John rested his hand on his son's shoulder. "He's worked too hard to not show off what he has."

Those damn tears rolled down her cheeks. "Is he registered?"

"Your grandfather took care of everything."

Kym covered her mouth and the cry had turned to a sob.

"The party."

"We brought the party with us. And everyone with us."

Abigail's sister and mother both smiled at her. She couldn't even believe she was standing there in that moment. But she'd never in her life been happier.

The competition progressed until it was time for Jacob to compete. Kym took him to the side.

"Are you ready for this?" she asked as she gave his belt knot a tug.

"I am, ma'am."

"There are a lot of kids here. All I ask is that you do your best."

"I will, ma'am."

She gave him a bow and he reciprocated. Then she pulled him into her arms for a hug. "I'm so proud of you."

When he pulled back he gave her a smile and lined up.

John moved in next to her and laced his arm around her waist.

"I didn't get to tell you that you did a great job."

She looked up at him. "You saw me?"

He nodded. "I wouldn't have missed it for the world."

Her heart was racing now, but it wasn't nerves that brought it on. It was the happiness that filled it completely.

Jacob was near the end of his competition and some of those kids knew what they were doing. Kym tried to keep calm as he introduced himself to the judges and then bowed.

Her stomach flopped and her muscles ached with each move he made—perfectly. How could John stand only a few feet from her with Cody asleep on his shoulder and not look nervous. She was a wild mass of nerves.

When Jacob was done and he turned while his scores were given, he looked at Kym and smiled. Her heart was nearly ready to explode. She'd loved John's kids since the second she'd met them, but in this very special moment she came to realize just how much.

The judges gave their scores and Kym wasn't even sure she heard them or saw them. She'd been paralyzed by Jacob's enormous smile.

"That puts him in first place," John said softly in her ear.

"Does it? I didn't know. I'm just so proud of him I could burst."

"Imagine how good that'll feel when you have your own kid out there."

She turned to him, her mouth open. What could she say to that?

"I feel like he is mine," she said.

"I think he is in spirit."

She smiled widely and turned back to watch them announce Jacob's first place win.

As Kym drove back home, the roads clean and dry, she looked at the boy next to her. Jacob had opted to ride home with her.

He slept in the passenger seat with both their first place trophies wrapped in his arms.

The sun had long ago tucked itself behind the mountains, but as she passed the cemetery she swore she could smell the flowers on a warm breeze in the car.

John waited by the front door as she climbed out of the car and a sleepy Jacob did the same.

"Kiddo, there is a pizza and a piece of cake on the table waiting for you," John said and Jacob gave him a nod as he carried his trophy into the house.

"He's exhausted."

"He worked hard for that."

"Yes he did."

John walked toward her. "I think Cody had the best birthday ever."

She smiled. "That makes me very happy."

"C'mon, there's pizza and cake waiting for you too."

With his arm around her waist she walked toward the house with him, but then he stopped.

"What's wrong?"

"I've been thinking, you're probably really tired tonight. Why don't you plan on not going home."

She pursed her lips. "That's not a good idea. You're kids…"

"Are expecting to find you waking up with me a lot in the future, but that's a conversation for tomorrow morning when we wake up."

He laced his arm around her again and escorted her into the house.

Epilogue

Sunday morning the sunshine was bright and Kym thought she could smell flowers in the air. She jumped when she felt John's arm wrap around her and for a moment she had to remind herself that she'd fallen asleep in his bed, in his home, in his arms.

"Good morning, my love," he whispered in her ear.

"Good morning."

The feel of him there made her long for it for the next morning and the next.

"I should go before the kids wake up."

He wrapped his arm tighter around her. "Oh, they're up and gone. My sister took them to church."

"Oh."

"It's just the two of us all day. I thought maybe we'd stay right here."

Kym rolled until she was facing him. "Do you really think that's wise?"

He nodded, his eyes closed and his face relaxed from sleep. "They're not coming home until dinner when we celebrate."

"Celebrate? What are you celebrating?"

"Oh, lots of things. Cody's birthday, your trophy, Jacob's trophy, our engagement." His eyes opened slowly and a smile formed on his lips.

Kym propped herself up on her elbow. "Our what?"

John rose to meet her. "Oh, I skipped a step."

"Yeah you did."

He reached his hand up and smoothed her hair. "I told you, you were the last woman I wanted to say I love you to."

"You did."

"I meant it. And I have four amazing and wonderful kids who love you too. They told me they did, when I asked them if I could marry you."

She pressed her fingers to her lips. "You asked them?"

He nodded and turned to reach for something off of the nightstand. "Here, they made these for you."

He handed her a stack of papers. "These are homemade cards." She could feel her eyes moisten.

"Congratulations cards. Look, Abby drew you next to your trophy."

"I love it." She looked back into his eyes and he moved in to kiss her gently.

"So I guess all that's left is to ask you if you'd bring that indomitable spirit into our house forever. Kym O'Bryne, will you marry me?"

Her pulse quickened and her chest felt full—full of love. "I've loved you since you crashed that silly grocery cart into me."

"You crashed into me."

She laughed. "I guess we can shop together now."

"Does that mean yes?"

She pressed a warm kiss to his lips. "That means yes."

We hope you enjoyed

Bernadette Marie's

Indomitable Spirit

Visit us again in
Aspen Creek
in the Fall of 2014
for
The Lost Ones

Meet the Author

Damon Kappel ©2009

Bestselling Author Bernadette Marie is known for building families readers want to be part of. Her series *The Keller Family* has graced bestseller charts since its release in 2011, along with her other series and single title books. The married mother of five sons promises *Happily Ever After always*...and says she can write it, because she lives it.

When not writing, Bernadette Marie is shuffling her sons to their many events—mostly hockey—and enjoying the beautiful views of the Colorado Rocky Mountains from her front step. She is also an accomplished martial artist with a second degree black belt in Tang Soo Do.

A chronic entrepreneur, Bernadette Marie opened her own publishing house in 2011, *5 Prince Publishing*, so that she could publish the books she liked to write and help make the dreams of other aspiring authors come true too.

Visit Bernadette Marie at www.bernadettemarie.com

Soul Connection *Doug Simpson*
Bridge Over the Atlantic *Lisa Hobman*
Unexpected Admirer *Bernadette Marie*
The Italian Job *Phyllis Humphrey*
Jaded *M.J. Kane*
Shades of Darkness *Melynda Price*
Heart like an Ocean *Christine Steendam*
The Depot *Carmen DeSousa*
Crisis of Identity *Denise Moncrief*
A Heart Broken *Sara Barnard*
Soul Mind *Doug Simpson*
Chunky Sugars *Sara Barnard*
When Noon day Ends *Carmen DeSousa*
Fatal Jealousy *Christina OW*
Center Stage *Bernadette Marie*
Chris Mouse and the Promise *Tina J Adams*
Soul Rescue *Doug Simpson*
The Pit Stop *Carmen DeSousa*
Soul Awakening *Doug Simpson*
First Kiss *Bernadette Marie*
A Heart Not Easily Broken *MJ Kane*
Entangled Dreams *Carmen DeSousa*
All for Love *Ann Swann*
Opposite Attraction *Bernadette Marie*
A Heart on Hold *Sara Barnard*
Petals *Rebekah Roberts*
Land of the Noonday Sun *Carmen DeSousa*
A Second Chance *Bernadette Marie*
Star Bright *Christina OW*
Until Darkness Comes *Melynda Price*
Candy Kisses *Bernadette Marie*
She Belongs to Me *Carmen DeSousa*
Cart before the Horse *Bernadette Marie*
The Executive Decision *Bernadette Marie*